This is Dinah the Mynah

She lives with Dad, Tammy and Mark.

DON'T MENTION THE HAIR

And this is Arnold Teabag, who helps save the family from terrible, awful, dreadful danger ...

Jeremy Strong once worked in a bakery, putting the jam into three thousand doughnuts every night. Now he puts the jam in stories instead, which he finds much more exciting. At the age of three, he fell out of a first-floor bedroom window and landed on his head. His mother says that this damaged him for the rest of his life and refuses to take any responsibility. He loves writing stories because he says it is 'the only time you alone have complete control and can make anything happen'. His ambition is to make you laugh (or at least snuffle). Jeremy Strong lives near Bath with his wife, Gillie, four cats and a flying cow.

Are you feeling silly enough to read more?

LAUGH YOUR SOCKS OFF WITH
Jeremy
STRONG

The Beak Speaks

Illustrated by Rowan Clifford

PUFFIN

PUFFIN BOOKS

Published by the Penguin Group
Penguin Books Ltd, 80 Strand, London WC2R 0RL, England
Penguin Group (USA) Inc., 375 Hudson Street, New York, New York 10014, USA
Penguin Group (Canada), 90 Eglinton Avenue East, Suite 700, Toronto, Ontario, Canada M4P 2Y3
(a division of Pearson Penguin Canada Inc.)
Penguin Ireland, 25 St Stephen's Green, Dublin 2, Ireland (a division of Penguin Books Ltd)
Penguin Group (Australia), 250 Camberwell Road, Camberwell, Victoria 3124, Australia
(a division of Pearson Australia Group Pty Ltd)
Penguin Books India Pvt Ltd, 11 Community Centre, Panchsheel Park, New Delhi – 110 017, India
Penguin Group (NZ), 67 Apollo Drive, Rosedale, Auckland 0632, New Zealand
(a division of Pearson New Zealand Ltd)
Penguin Books (South Africa) (Pty) Ltd, Block D, Rosebank Office Park, 181 Jan Smuts Avenue,
Parktown North, Gauteng 2193, South Africa

Penguin Books Ltd, Registered Offices: 80 Strand, London WC2R 0RL, England

puffinbooks.com

First published in Puffin Books 2003
This edition published 2012
001 – 10 9 8 7 6 5 4 3 2 1

Text copyright © Jeremy Strong, 2003
Illustrations copyright © Rowan Clifford, 2003
All rights reserved

The moral right of the author and illustrator has been asserted

Set in Baskerville MT
Printed in Great Britain by Clays Ltd, St Ives plc

British Library Cataloguing in Publication Data
A CIP catalogue record for this book is available from the British Library

ISBN: 978-0-141-33619-0

With thanks to Mirjana, Srdjan and Andrija,
for all their hospitality and friendship

Contents

DARKUSS!
DARKUSS!

1 Dinah: Sausage Dogs and Custard

Dogs! Useless creatures. Brains like porridge. And the one at the vet's clinic was an excellent example of just how useless a dog could be.

When I saw that bit of plastic water pipe I laughed so much I nearly fell out of my bird cage. The tube had been brought in by a spotty girl and she placed it carefully on the examination table.

'What have we got here?' asked Mr Peter. (He's the vet and my hero. Oh yes, just you wait and see!)

'It's me dog,' the girl answered with a sniff. (It wasn't an upset kind of sniff – more of a sniffy sniff, like her nose was blocked and she didn't have a hanky.)

'A dog?' mused Mr Peter, and there was a muffled 'wuff' from deep inside.

The girl nodded. 'Ran in there after a rabbit, didn't she? Rabbit came out the other end, but the dog didn't. Stuck in there, isn't she?' Sniff.

That sniffing was getting on my nerves. I wanted to shove one wing under her nose and say, 'For heaven's sake, blow!' But Mr Peter was all patience.

'Shouldn't be too much of a problem,' he said, lifting one end of the tube and peering down it.

Sniff. 'That's 'er back end.'

'So I see,' said Mr Peter. 'Good thing I've had five years of training to spot things like that. OK, here is what I'm going to do. This is a bottle of cooking oil. I'm going to dribble this down the inside lining of the tube to make it nice and slippery like so, and we leave it a few moments for the oil to work right the way down. There we are, and now we give the tube a little shake and whoops! Out comes Fido!'

''Er name's Chantelle,' sniffed the girl.

Chantelle? Ooh la la! Manky Mophead would

have been a better name. Do you know what came out of that tube? It wasn't a dog. It was a long, thin mess of tangled, slimy fur that just so happened to have four tiddly legs, a silly tiddly head at one end and an excuse for a tiddly tail at the other. It was a long-haired dachshund – you know, a sausage dog – and boy, did it look daft! Oh yes!

But then dogs are often like that, aren't they? They've no pride, no sense of style at all. Me, I'm the Style Queen.

It's because I'm a mynah bird. Mynah birds have natural finesse. *Finesse* – that's French, you know. It means good taste and elegance. I'm well educated, you see – I speak a bit of French, a bit of English – shows how cultured I am. Mynah birds are famous for speaking well, and I'm one of the best.

'Good evening, sir. Dinner will be served in the dining-cage at eight.' See? That's posh talk, that is. Mynahs don't do any of that awful screechy-squawky ''Allo!' business you get from parrots. Parrots are rubbish, but mynah birds, we're something different. We've got style. Oh yes.

Unlike this dachshund, which was slithering about on the table trying to stand up but failing because every surface was covered with cooking oil. I couldn't help laughing. Well, it was funny! I was in hysterics, hanging upside down from my perch and banging my head on the cage floor.

'I have done many strange things in my animal clinic,' explained Mr Peter, 'but I've never had to shake a dog out of a tube before.'

The girl sniffed again and tried to pick up Chantelle. 'Urgh. She's all gunky.'

'Wipe her over with a towel when you get home. She'll be as right as rain in no time. Just don't let her fall on the barbecue.'

'What?'

'Joke,' explained Mr Peter.

'Joke?' Sniff.

'Never mind,' sighed Mr Peter. 'Bye-bye.'

'Wuff,' said the dog.

'Don't swear,' said Mr Peter. I was on my back in my cage, kicking my legs in the air and screaming with laughter. The girl glanced across at me.

'That bird all right or is she choking on something?'

'Dinah likes to show off,' said Mr Peter.

The liar! The great big liar! I do NOT show off. AND I HATE BEING CALLED DINAH! What a daft name. Dinah the Mynah, I ask you! I could see that dachshund smirking at me too. Stupid dog.

I hate dogs. They think they're so clever, just because they can run and jump and fetch sticks and stuff. I mean, what use is that? Just suppose I went flying off, got a stick and brought it back for you. I put it down at your feet and I say, 'There you are, I've brought you a stick, look.'

And you'd say: 'What do I want a stick for?'

And I'd say: 'I dunno.'

And you'd say: 'I dunno, either. Go and put it back.'

You see what I mean? What are sticks *for*? They're for trees, that's what. Trees have sticks on them and what I say is, leave them there. Dogs are just stupid.

Mr Peter's a good vet. I owe my life to him. He saved me from almost certain death. Oh yes. My previous life was terrible. I was being held prisoner by animal smugglers. They kept all these animals locked away in stinking cages, waiting to be sold. Like slaves, we were. I managed to escape from my cage, but I couldn't get out of the room. Want to know what they used to catch me? A vacuum cleaner.

That's right! They sucked me right up it. SHLOPP! I disappeared backwards up the tube. Have you ever heard a squawk in reverse? It goes sort of KWAUQS! Sounded like I'd swallowed a cork. It took off most of my feathers. But when they opened up the machine I skedaddled like my bottom was on fire! I whizzed out through the door and took to the air.

It was a nightmare. My feathers were falling out all the time and I

KWAUQS!!!

was losing power and eventually I just couldn't keep going. I went into a nosedive (actually it was more of a beak-dive) and – *Spladdash!* – I plunged straight into Mr Peter's garden pond. That was a stroke of luck!

He rescued me. I didn't have many feathers left. I was all in the nuddy, and me the Style Queen! The shame of it. But the feathers grew back eventually and he's looked after me ever since. I still have nightmares about that other place, but I'm safe now, with Mr Peter and his children.

Mark and Tamsin are great. They give me loads of nibbly things to eat when Mr Peter isn't looking, and they let me out of the cage much more than he does.

Mark's the oldest. He takes life very seriously, but he looks like an idiot – and I mean that in the nicest possible way. You can never be sure what he's going to appear as. He's mad about animals, like his dad. He spent all last week pretending he was an archerfish, squirting jets of water at flies. He got soaked. Tammy got soaked. I got soaked. Mr Peter got soaked . . . and then rather cross.

This week Mark is busy being a leopard. He's dyed his blond hair with leopard spots. He goes creeping about the place, sneaking behind the chairs and then pouncing on people.

Mr Peter spilled his dinner last night when Mark suddenly ambushed him from under the table. Mr Peter was not pleased, surprise, surprise.

'I'm a leopard, Dad. I've got to practise my hunting skills.'

'Well, now you can be a leopard cleaning the carpet.'

'I don't think leopards clean carpets in the wild,' Mark pointed out.

'Well, if this leopard doesn't clean this carpet, this leopard is going to be in very big trouble. Does this leopard understand?'

So the leopard cleaned the carpet.

But the real reason why Mark is so serious, despite his leopard-spot hair, is because of his dad, Mr Peter. (Full name: Peter Draper, Veterinary Surgeon, of the Small Paws Animal Clinic – there, now you've been properly introduced.) Mark and Tammy haven't got a mum, you see. She went off to America with someone else. Mr Peter says she flew there, but he must be making that up. She had such thin arms – she'd never even have taken off, let alone flown. Ha ha. Mynah joke.

Mark and Tamsin only get to see her about once a year. They were pretty cut up about it, but they've settled down a lot. It happened about two years ago and now Mark reckons he's got to look after his dad. He talks to me a lot, you see – that's how I know. He says he's second-in-command.

'There's nobody else to look after him,' he told me. 'It's all down to me, and I know what's wrong.' He thinks I don't understand what he says, but of course I do. I mean, I don't just have style, I'm intelligent too.

I just looked at him. Sometimes it's best to keep quiet, especially if you're a bird. People don't expect you to say anything too brainy. If you do, they come over all funny. I kept quiet and waited to hear what he'd say next.

'What Dad needs is a girlfriend.'

'SQUAAA$**&%*WKKK!'

OK, so maybe that wasn't a very intelligent thing to say, but I was shocked. I was thinking, hang on, chum, you can't go around picking up girlfriends for people, especially not for your own dad! But Mark was serious. I couldn't believe it.

'He can share his work with her and he'll have someone to talk to. Tammy can have a new mum and she can come and live here and she can make custard without lumps for us, because Dad's always has lumps in it, Dinah, you know it does.'

That last bit was true enough, but I still thought it was a bit much. Just because you don't want lumps in your custard doesn't mean you can go round grabbing girlfriends for your dad, does it? Anyhow, what was Mark planning to do? Was he going to put all girlfriends through a custard-making test before he allowed them anywhere near his dad?

The thing is, when Mark gets serious about something it's time to watch out. Every now and then he gets these Bright Ideas, and if it's not Mark thinking of something, it's that crazy friend of his, Sanjeev. (It was Sanjeev who put the leopard spots on Mark's hair.) The problem is that Mark's bright ideas nearly always lead to trouble.

And this latest idea was not simply going to lead us into trouble. It was going to take us straight to The Dark House, the most terrifying place I have ever seen. It was a return to all my old nightmares.

I mean, we all nearly DIED!

2 Mark: How to Organize Dad

I'm going to be a vet when I grow up, like my dad. He's fantastic. He stopped a lion coughing once. Can you imagine trying to cure a lion of *anything*? I'd have been scared stiff, but my dad, he just went straight up to it and said, 'Open up, chum!' And the lion opened its mouth and Dad tipped a spoonful of cough medicine down its throat and then came home. It's true; Dad told me.

I think working with sick animals is a great job. Sometimes Dad brings the smaller animals home and Tammy and I help look after them. That's how we got our mynah bird. Almost all her feathers had come off. She almost died, but Dad saved her. We call her Dinah and she goes everywhere with us. Dad's always talking to her. Mynahs are terrific at learning words and Dad has taught her loads. He takes her into the surgery with him and sometimes I go too and help him. It's all part of my plan to become a vet like him.

I reckon that if you want to do something in life, then you've got to get yourself organized. It's no good waiting for it to happen. I've already started practising to be a vet. I've often watched Dad at work and I've picked up loads of information from him. And I like to actually try and be different animals, so that I can understand how they think and feel. I've read tons of books too – hundreds and thousands, I expect.

My friends at school are always bringing in animals for me to sort out. Last week Jade brought me a robin with a stuck beak, and

Sanjeev is always bringing me problems. Yesterday he had two worms that had tied themselves together in knots. Actually, Sanjeev brings me so many animal problems I sometimes think that he's deliberately testing me or something. Anyhow, I get lots of practice.

When I get older I'm going to be a proper vet and I shall give cough medicine to sick lions (if I'm brave enough) and mend elephants and stick broken ostriches back together and things like that. I shall probably travel the world, looking after animals.

My dad's the best vet there is, but he works too hard. He's always rushing around, seeing to sick animals, and when he's not doing that he's coming to school to pick me up, or taking Tammy to playgroup or the childminder. He never stops.

And he's lonely. I just know he is. He's only got me and Tammy now. I watch him sometimes, when he thinks he's by himself. I keep an eye on him and, to tell you the truth, sometimes I think he's going a bit mad with the loneliness. I often hear him talking to himself – at least that's what I *thought* it was and then I realized he was talking to Dinah the Mynah. How weird is that?

He doesn't just teach her words – he *talks* to her, like she's a real person, almost like she's his wife or something. He tells her what he's been doing, and how me and Tammy are doing at school, and how he cut himself cooking, and the state of Tammy's socks and all the sort of useless rubbishy stuff that he used to talk about with Mum, until she went off.

Dinah the Mynah sits there cackling and nodding as if she understands everything he says. Definitely weird.

So I reckon that what Dad really, really needs is a girlfriend. Then he can marry her and she can come and live here and he'll have someone to talk to and he'll be happy.

It was my teacher who gave me the idea. Miss Pettigrew is quite nice, even though she's about a hundred years old. She's retiring at the end of this year. She keeps telling us that we are her 'very last class', and she seems ever so cheerful. But she *will* make us do Country Dancing.

I hate Country Dancing. Miss Pettigrew goes

to an Irish dancing club and she makes us do it as well. We have to stand there with our arms quite still and make our legs flip about all over the place. Sanjeev always manages to fall over and knock down everyone else. We end up looking like some sort of World Champion Pick-Up-Sticks Competition. I think he does it deliberately.

Anyhow, Miss Pettigrew was marking my maths and out of the blue she asked me how my father was getting on. 'Is he still on his own?'

'He's got Tammy and me,' I said.

'I bet you and Tammy look after him very

well too. But your father is such a good-looking man. Doesn't he have a lady in his life?'

'A girlfriend?'

Miss Pettigrew coughed. 'I think "girlfriend" sounds a bit young. He needs an older woman. I thought that by now he might have a lady he likes.'

I shook my head and Miss Pettigrew didn't say any more about it. But I was already thinking. Miss Pettigrew was right. Dad *should* have a lady friend. He *needed* a lady friend. But how on earth could he find one?

Sanjeev suggested the local newspaper. It comes out once a week and it has a Lonely Hearts column. He brought one to school to show me.

'There are loads of messages from men and women looking for friends. Here's one:

Lady, bubbly redhead, stunningly attractive, 35, wishes to meet handsome, rich man, GSOH, with houses in France and Jamaica.'

'What does a lady with a bubbling red head look like?' I asked. 'She sounds like a Martian. Anyhow, I'll never be able to persuade Dad to write to someone himself. I'd have to put an advert in for him. What sorts of things do the ads say?'

'How about this?' Sanjeev began.

'**Gentleman,** 75, GSOH, enjoys fast wheelchairs, seeks lovely lady with own old people's home.'

'Why do they keep saying GSOH? What does that mean?'

'I think it's a short way of saying Good Set Of Hair,' Sanjeev explained.

And that was how my neat idea was born. I talked to Tammy about it and she thought it was great. I had to swear her to secrecy. I said that if she told anyone, her teddy's eyes would fall out, so she's taken it very seriously.

The biggest problem was how to pay for the ad. I had a little pocket money, but I had to earn the rest of the money as best I could, and that meant washing Dad's Land Rover.

I hate washing the Land Rover. It gets filthy outside AND in. Dad has to put animals inside, and sometimes they throw up or have a wee or worse, and they leave their hair all over the place and it just STINKS.

I did that for about a month, although it felt more like a year, until I had the money, and then Tammy and I sat down and we wrote an ad for Dad.

Peter, 34, tall, dark, handsome vet, GSOH, is looking for a nice lady to come and look after him. Small Paws Animal Clinic.

Tammy nodded and stuck her thumb in her mouth. 'What does "handsome" mean?' she asked.

'Good looking.'

'His ears stick out,' said Tamsin.

'No, they don't!'

'They do, like a donkey.'

'You mean a monkey.'

Tammy shook her head seriously. 'Like a donkey,' she insisted, and her eyes grew really wide and she whispered loudly. 'Daddy's ears are HUGE.'

'No, they're not!'

'And he's got hairy toes,' Tammy declared with a frown. 'I wouldn't marry anyone with hairy toes. I'm going to marry Robbie at playgroup and he hasn't got hairy toes.'

'You're too young to marry,' I snapped. 'Look, can we get back to the advert?'

'Will the lady be pretty?'

'I don't know. We haven't seen her yet.'

'Will she be my mummy?'

'Would you like that?'

Tammy thought for a long time and then asked if the lady liked Sugar Pops. Sugar Pops is her favourite breakfast cereal.

'She might.'

'Well, if she does, I think I'll like her but if she doesn't, then she's probably a witch because witches can't eat Sugar Pops. It makes them explode. Robbie told me.'

I gave up. How could I talk about such important matters to a four-year-old who thinks her dad's ears are like a donkey's and tells you that witches can't eat Sugar Pops in case they explode? You can see why I have to do all the organizing. I took the letter down to the post box and shoved it in.

3 Dinah: Too Many Ladies in Waiting

Oh – is it my turn again? I was nodding off there.
Mark does go on a bit. Hang on a sec while I get
this feather straight. Got to keep up a good
appearance, you know. Now, where was I? Oh
yes. I was telling you about Mark's Bright Ideas.
This is a typical one, OK? It happened about a
month ago. Mr Peter and I were over in the
clinic. He likes my company. (Who wouldn't?) My
cage goes in the corner of the surgery.

Anyhow, we'd finished at the surgery and Mr
Peter was carrying me back to the house. On the
way there we heard this distant shouting.

'Help! Dad! Get me down!'

We looked up and there, right near the top of
a tree, was Mark, clinging on to a branch. He
was stuck. Not only that, but for some odd
reason he had a TV aerial strapped to his head.
Mr Peter was gobsmacked.

He had to call out the fire brigade, and while we were waiting he began asking Mark why he had a TV aerial strapped to his head.

'It's for the rabbit,' said Mark.

Well, there's an answer for you! We should have known, shouldn't we? It was for the rabbit. How stupid of us not to realize! I wanted to scream at him – *What do you mean, it's for the rabbit? What rabbit?*

Luckily, Mr Peter more or less screamed it for me. '*What rabbit?*'

'The one in the hutch on the lawn. He looked really bored, Dad, and I thought, the rabbit can watch TV. Then he'll have something to do.'

'But the rabbit hasn't got a TV.'

'He has. I put one in his hutch this afternoon, but I couldn't get a good picture on it and I thought I'd put the aerial higher. I couldn't climb and carry the aerial, so I put it on my head and now I'm stuck. Get me down, Dad, please.'

Mr Peter stood there, shaking his head. I sat there on my perch, shaking my head. That's Mark for you – he's always doing things like that.

And then there's Tamsin. If you think Mark is odd, you should meet Tamsin. She does make me laugh! She's only four but she's got more energy than a nuclear power station.

Come to think of it, you remember I said it was because of Mark that we nearly died? Well, actually it was both of them. It was partly because Mark was trying to fix Mr Peter up with a girlfriend, and partly because Tamsin kept annoying her childminder. She came back one afternoon and Mr Peter asked her what she'd done that day.

'I made a crockadipe from an egg box and Nasha helped me paint it,' she said.

'Lovely. Have you brought the crocodile home?'

'No, cos I put it in a bowl of water and the paint came off and the water went green and the crockadipe went all soggy and fell to bits and Nasha was cross.'

'Oh dear. Why was that?'

Tamsin shrugged her little shoulders. 'I don't know,' she grumbled.

'It wasn't a bowl of water, Dad,' explained Mark. 'It was a fruit salad that Natasha was making for supper. The paint came off in the fruit juice and the egg box fell to bits. Natasha ended up with a bowl of fruit slices and soggy cardboard lumps all slopping about in green paint. She had to throw it away.'

'No wonder she was cross.'

'Nasha said I was more trouble than a box of monkeys!' Tammy boasted. (That's certainly true.)

Mr Peter seemed annoyed that Tammy had caused so much trouble, but he couldn't help smiling. 'I don't think you should be so proud of being a monkey,' he began, but Tammy butted in.

'Not one monkey, Daddy, lots of monkeys – a whole boxful, a big box, a big, Big, BIG box as big as a brontosorepuss!'

I think Tamsin is so clever. Fancy making a crocodile from egg boxes! What a good idea. If only ALL crocodiles were made from egg boxes – there'd be no trouble with them at all, would there? They'd be just about to lunge at you with their snappy jaws all full of teeth and death and then, just before they got you, they'd go all soggy and fall to bits in the water.

'Oh dear,' they'd say. 'I'm a floppy-crocky. Boo hoo.'

The next day was even worse. I'm not exactly sure what happened, but it had something to do with one of those elastic ropes with a hook at each end. Apparently Tamsin had fastened two of her friends together, back to back, through the window of the playhouse. Clever girl! She's brilliant! So now there was a toddler on either side and neither of them could get away. They were pushing and pulling and yelling and screaming and eventually the whole lot came tumbling down.

Natasha said she couldn't take Tam any longer. She was too much trouble. Boo! Hiss! Measly old Natasha – what a fuss about nothing! She was only having fun. But it meant that Mr

Peter no longer had a childminder. He would have to look after Tamsin himself.

All this happened just as the Lonely Hearts advert came out in the paper. Oh yes, Mark had told me all about it. I said I didn't think it was a good idea, but of course he didn't understand me. Humans are so dense. I've no idea why we can understand them, but they have no idea what we're saying. Personally, I think it's the schools and the teachers. It's all very well teaching them maths and stuff, but why can't they learn Mynah Bird? It's not difficult. I've been speaking it since I was a baby. Ha ha. Mynah joke again.

Anyhow, all of a sudden there's a phone call from Julie. She's Mr Peter's assistant at the clinic and she had just opened up for the morning.

'You'd better come round at once, Peter. I don't know what's going on. The waiting room is jam-packed, and they're all women,' she explained. 'They don't seem to have any pets with them or anything. It's just – women!'

Of course, I knew exactly what was going on and so did Mark, but poor Mr Peter – he had no idea at all. He started muttering, 'Work,

work, work, work, work.' He grabbed my cage
and we hurried round to the clinic. The place
was heaving! It was wall-to-wall women, in
every size, shape and age.

'They were queuing outside when I arrived,'
Julie began. 'They waved newspapers at me.
Something is going on, but don't ask me what
it is.'

'All right, I'll sort it out. Julie, can you look
after Tamsin today and watch the desk here?
The childminder won't take her any more. Can
you do that – just today, please? Please?' Mr
Peter was desperate.

Julie rolled her eyes. Honestly, you'd have
thought he was asking her to jump inside a
crockadipe, but she said she'd do it. 'But I'm not
sorting out this lot,' she added, pointing at the
crowded waiting room. 'They're all yours.'

The women stared at Mr Peter, looking him
up and down. Poor man! He had no idea what
he was in for.

'Are you Peter?' murmured one lady, in a
sweet-as-honey voice.

He coughed nervously. 'Yes?'

'I'm Rowena.' The lady with the honey voice

pushed forward, fluttering her long false eyelashes until one fell off, much to the amusement of the others. What a dreadful performance – no style at all.

'And my name is Rachel,' said another. She grasped Mr Peter's hand, shaking it and shaking it. 'My goodness, what warm hands you have. Are you warm all over?'

They began to crowd round him, wanting to shake his hand or touch his arm. Mr Peter was stuck in the middle, turning bright red and trying to make himself thinner and thinner, and wishing he could disappear.

These women had all answered the Lonely Hearts ad. They were eyeing him up! I was beginning to enjoy this, and I thought that maybe I could help.

'Custard!' I cried. 'Make custard!'

'Shut up, Dinah,' hissed Mark, while the clamouring ladies closed in on his dad.

'I'm Lindy.'

'Perry.'

'Excuse me, I'm Sharon and I was here before you.'

'You were not!'

'I was so!'

They started pushing at each other, trying to get to the front of the crowd.

'Ow! You're treading on my feet!' complained one lady, who I thought looked rather like Miss Pettigrew, even though she was almost unrecognizable behind a large pair of sunglasses. I knew her from the time Mark took me into school.

'Well, they shouldn't be so big. Besides, old-age pensioners like you should be banned.'

'How dare you!'

'Will you get your elbow out of my chest?'

'Ouch! I'll get you for that, you little monster!'

'Make custard!' I cried again. I slipped upside down and began banging my head on the floor of my cage, it was so funny.

But they didn't want to make custard and they began fighting instead. Then somebody's big blonde wig went flying across the clinic like a terrified Persian cat in for neutering.

'Ow! My hair!'

Arms and legs were waving and kicking all over the place. Shoes went zooming through the air. Handbags were furiously whirled and twirled, occasionally making very loud thuds as they connected with a target, which would immediately let out an even louder yell.

Mr Peter forced his way across to the reception desk and climbed on top. He opened his mouth, took a deep breath and roared at the top of his voice.

'STOP THIS AT ONCE!'

The wriggling, writhing heap of bodies on the floor of the clinic froze, just as if someone had pressed the STOP button on a video machine. Everyone stared at him.

'How dare you come into my clinic and behave like wild animals!' he bellowed. 'Only wild animals are allowed to behave like, um, wild animals!'

What a daft thing to say! I expect Mr Peter

was feeling a bit put out. He tried to sound stern. 'Someone tell me what this is all about, quietly, or I shall call the police!'

Sharon pulled a rather torn newspaper from her handbag and pointed to one page. 'It's the advert,' she declared peevishly.

'What advert?'

'The one you put in the paper, in the Lonely Hearts column,' chorused the women.

'The one I . . .?' Mr Peter's voice trailed off. He had just caught sight of Mark. Uh-oh!

'Mark! Was this another of your Bright Ideas?'

'Sort of,' said Mark.

'What do you mean, sort of?'

'Sort of – yes. I did it, but Sanjeev thought of it.'

'Sanjeev,' groaned Mr Peter. 'I might have known.'

Mark slipped behind one of the clamouring ladies. I think he was taking cover.

'Is this your son?' crooned the lady. 'Isn't he sweet!'

'No, he isn't,' growled Mr Peter. 'He's an interfering wotsit! Now, get out of my surgery – all of you. Go on – shoo! Scat!'

He waved his arms at the women and they backed off like scared mice. Mr Peter saw them out through the door of the clinic and slammed it shut with a sigh of relief. He took a deep breath, turned round and almost jumped out of his skin.

4 Mark: The Madwoman from Romania

I could see Dad was surprised. So was I. One
woman had stayed behind. Now she rose to her
feet. She seemed to glitter as she moved. Her
clothes were deeply coloured – dark red velvets,
gold brocades and emerald satins. A scarf,
threaded with gold and silver, was draped round
her neck and over one shoulder. Her arms
jangled with bracelets and bangles. Delicate
silver earrings dangled from her ears. Her hair
seemed to encircle her head like some dense,
black galaxy.

She smiled at Dad as she crossed the room
towards him, slipping one arm through his and
pulling him towards a chair, so that he could sit
down. She smiled again and spoke in a throaty,
foreign voice, making her r's growl.

'Come, Mr Vetman, sit down, you have had
shock . . .'

'I'm still having one,' Dad murmured.

'Make custard.' This was Dinah the Mynah. Sometimes she gets words stuck in her tiny brain and keeps repeating them.

'My name – Miriana. I from Romania. I nice lady like it say here.' Miriana pointed to the advert. 'Now I make you cup of coffee and I stay and I look after you and this little man and everyone is happy. No?'

Little man! Honestly, she made me sound like a garden gnome!

She smiled again at Dad and suddenly flicked a sour glance at Julie. 'Now I am here she can go home,' Miriana announced, curling her lip. 'She too young, like girl.' Miriana fixed Dad with her dark eyes and growled at him. 'I woman!'

Dad was speechless. He seemed to have turned into a statue. He just sat there, staring into the dark pools of her eyes. At last he found his voice.

'Now listen, Miss . . . um, Mrs . . .?'

'My name Miriana. I am good for you!' She flung both arms round him. Dad turned bright red and he tried to grapple with her, but she was like an octopus, clinging to him. I didn't know what to do. I didn't know whether to pull her off, or what.

'I make you happy!' crooned Miriana.

'I AM happy!' Dad roared furiously. 'Will you get off me? Now go! Go! I don't want a girlfriend!'

Miriana's eyes widened. 'Oh no,' she said, shaking her head. 'I not your girlfriend.'

'No, you're not. I'm glad we agree on that,' snapped Dad.

'I not your girlfriend. I your wife. I be your wife and you be Mr Vetman and I be Mrs Vetman and we have lots of children and we live, how you say? Happy ever forever.'

'Make custard!' Dinah ordered. She seemed to have custard on the brain.

'Shut up, you crazy bird!' yelled Dad, leaping to

his feet. 'And you, get out of my surgery! This is not a dating agency. It's an animal clinic. Go on, get out!'

But Miriana was not going to give up easily. 'You want sick animal? I bring sick animal. You wait, I come back.' Miriana reached the door. She flashed a charming smile. 'Happy ever forever,' she growled, and then she vanished.

Dad spun round and stared at me with a face full of thunder. I suddenly got this sickening feeling in the pit of my stomach. He clamped one hand on my shoulder, grabbed Dinah's cage and steered me back to the house. I didn't think we were going to end up happy forever at all.

I don't know why Dad had to blow his top about the advert. I was only trying to get him organized. It's not my fault he can't see that he needs a girlfriend. Sometimes I think he's more of a child than I am, and I'm more grown-up than he is. He might at least have given those ladies half a chance. He could have interviewed them or something. But no, Dad had to send them all packing, so I don't suppose they'll ever come back.

Dad was cross about it all weekend. Almost

every time we met he hissed at me, 'No girlfriends!' Then there'd be a seething pause. 'And tell Sanjeev to keep his ideas to himself.' Another simmering pause. 'And tell him to leave your hair alone!'

It was quite a relief to get back to the peace and quiet of school on Monday. I told Sanjeev what had happened and all about the Madwoman from Romania. I've got a funny feeling about her. She's weird.

Sanjeev reckoned it was all too much for him. 'It's because there were so many of them. He was probably scared.'

'Don't be stupid! My dad's poured cough medicine down a lion's throat. He's not scared of anything.'

Sanjeev suddenly grinned from ear to ear. 'I know! Why don't we raffle him?'

'Raffle Dad? How do you mean?'

'We make him top prize in a raffle, we sell tickets and the winning ticket gets your dad.'

'Suppose the winning ticket goes to a man? Or suppose it goes to some really horrible old lady with no teeth and a hairy chin and wobbly legs?'

Sanjeev went all moody. 'You're always picking holes in my ideas,' he said, and then brightened up again. 'Do you fancy being a vulture?'

'What?'

'I could shave off your hair, so you're all bald. Vultures are bald. It's so they can fly faster. If I shave your hair off, you'll be able to run faster. You'll be able to run a million miles an hour.'

'Sanjeev, you are talking complete rubbish. Vultures have a bald head and neck, so they don't get blood all over their feathers when they're feeding.'

Sanjeev kicked a stone. 'Think you know everything about animals, don't you?'

'I know that,' I told him, because I did. I remembered reading about it.

We were saved from further quarrelling by Nathan. He had brought me a patient and we went into the empty classroom to examine it.

'It's a mouse with a bent tail,' he said, holding out a small box.

Before I could stop him he took off the lid and it leaped out. The mouse went zooming away with the three of us in hot pursuit.

'Catch it before Miss Pettigrew gets here!' yelled Sanjeev.

'Catch what before Miss Pettigrew gets here?' asked Miss Pettigrew. How come teachers *always* walk in when you really don't want them to?

'Stand still, boys. No rushing about in the classroom. What's all this about?'

Nathan has got as much nerve as a rabbit being questioned by a shark. He blurted out the whole story.

'There's a mouse loose in the classroom? Then we'd better catch it before everyone else gets here. Oh dear, I'm so glad you're my last class.'

We began hunting around and when I moved the paint trolley, the mouse whizzed away.

'Watch out, Miss Pettigrew, it's coming your way!'

'Oh! Oh!'

Talk about Irish dancing! Miss Pettigrew was THE champion! Her feet were a blur. Her legs were snipping and snapping like chopsticks. The amazing thing was that it didn't scare the mouse at all. In fact, it seemed positively attracted by all that movement. It made a beeline – or should I say, a mouseline – straight for Miss Pettigrew, dashed on to her foot and vanished up her trousers!

'OH! OH! OH!'

Miss Pettigrew began leaping even higher. She made a grab at her shin. 'I've got it, I've got – oh! It's gone again. Quick, somebody help!'

How on earth were we supposed to help her? What could we do? We just stood there, goggling at our dancing teacher.

'I have it!' Miss Pettigrew was clutching her thigh. The mouse wriggled and it was off again, climbing even higher. It disappeared round behind her and Miss Pettigrew suddenly grabbed at her bottom.

'Oh, oh! I can't bear it! I shall have to take off these trousers!'

Still clutching her bottom, Miss Pettigrew shuffled down the corridor and into the girls' toilet. She pulled the door shut. There was an awful lot of banging, the door opened a tiny crack and her hand appeared, dangling the trousers.

'Mark, make absolutely sure there is NO mouse in those trousers. Then hand them back to me, and for goodness' sake be quick!'

I shook the trousers as hard as I could.

That was when the head teacher appeared. Miss Pettigrew was yelling from inside, 'Give those trousers back quickly!' Her hand waved from behind the door. I was brandishing Miss Pettigrew's trousers and, strange to say, he wondered what was going on.

It took fifteen minutes of explaining by four different people. Even then I am not too sure whether Mr Raza believed us. However, he did find it very funny. (I didn't.) He told the entire staff at lunchtime. Poor Miss Pettigrew had to put up with no end of jokes, and so did I. We never found the mouse with the bent tail. I hope it's all right.

At the end of the day Miss Pettigrew asked if she could have a quick word with Dad. She must have seen my face. 'It's all right, Mark, I would just like to tell him the story before he hears it from somewhere else. I want to make sure that you don't get into any more trouble.'

I thought that was really nice of her, so I got Dad and we sat in the classroom while Miss Pettigrew told her tale. I told my side too, just to make things clear.

'I'm very sorry it happened at all,' sighed Dad, giving me a long-suffering look.

'Oh, I have to admit I felt cross at the time, standing there in the toilet with nothing . . .' Both Dad and Miss Pettigrew grew rather red and Miss Pettigrew hurried on.

'I mean, the mouse; I've never liked mice. I'm quite happy with spiders, but I don't like scampery things.' Miss Pettigrew smiled again. 'How about you, Mr Draper?' she asked. 'Are you managing? Did you see anyone you liked on Saturday?'

How did Miss Pettigrew know about Saturday? Dad was looking puzzled too and as for my teacher, I had never seen her so flustered.

'What about Saturday?' asked Dad.

'I was . . . I mean . . . I think someone told me some ladies came to see you.'

'Yes. They'd made a mistake,' frowned Dad.

'I sometimes think an older woman can bring the right touch,' Miss Pettigrew offered. 'To the children, I mean. Naturally. But don't you miss the company?'

'What sort of company?'

'I thought, maybe, sometimes, perhaps you felt, you know, um . . . lonely? I know I get lonely sometimes, being on my own,' said Miss Pettigrew, rushing on. 'I mean, sometimes I'm lonely and sometimes I'm not; happy as a lamb sometimes, most of the time, and then other times . . .' Her voice trailed away.

I was beginning to think that my ancient teacher was flirting with my own dad, but that would have been totally crazy!

'I don't have time to get lonely. I have two

children to look after – two interfering children, I might add, especially one of them.' Dad looked at me again. This long-suffering look of his was getting a bit worn out, if you ask me.

Miss Pettigrew reached out and gently laid a hand on Dad's arm. 'Even so, the company of children does become a bit wearing after a while. I should know! I do think adults need the company of other adults, don't you?'

Dad rose to his feet, looking a little flustered. 'Come on, Mark, time to go home. We have to collect Tammy.'

Just as we were leaving, I caught a flicker of movement out of the corner of my eye. It was up on the window sill and then in a flash it was gone. It all happened so quickly that I wasn't even sure I had seen it at all. It was the mouse. I was about to tell Dad and Miss Pettigrew, but I was getting really hungry for tea and we'd already stayed on after school. Dad was tugging me on the arm – he seemed to be in a hurry to escape too. So I kept quiet, and, in fact, things more or less stayed quiet for the rest of the week. Thank goodness for that.

5 Dinah: Introducing Arnold

Quiet? What about Saturday morning? I mean, you really don't expect a chimpanzee to come crashing down the chimney at three o'clock on a Saturday morning, do you? That's not exactly quiet, is it?

There I was, snoozing the night away in the front room, when all of a sudden there's this whooshing, scraping noise, a cloud of soot comes flying out of the fireplace (putting black spots all over my yellow wattles, I might add) and a moment later a chimpanzee is sitting there.

The soot got up my beak. I sneezed so hard I did a reverse spin on my perch and fell off. I felt so undignified, lying there with my legs waving in the air. I struggled back on to my perch and tried to look nonchalant, but interesting.

The chimpanzee just sat in the fireplace, holding out his left arm and gazing at it intently. 'I've broken my arm,' he said mournfully. 'Look.'

He lifted it a little
and the front half
hung down.
He pushed it
with his
other hand
and it
swung from
one side to
the other.
'You see? It's
broken there, right in
the middle.'

'That's your elbow,' I said.

His head jerked up and he looked at me with
such joy. 'Really? Do you really think so? It's not
broken?'

'It's definitely your elbow,' I said, and I was
thinking, This chimp's an idiot.

Almost as if he wanted to prove my point, the
chimp now lifted his right arm and made that
one swing backwards and forwards too. He was
delighted.

'Look! Look! The other one does the same
thing! I've got *two* elbows!'

'Congratulations,' I muttered, while the chimp sat in the fireplace making both arms swing at once and blissfully beaming at them.

I shall let you into a secret. I have often sat in my cage, all alone, and wondered, Wouldn't it be nice if I had a companion? Someone I could talk with. We could muse upon the state of the world. We could chat about fashion and how to get the glossiest feathers and how to strut with style. What fun that would be! It was a lovely, comforting kind of thought.

And who do I get to talk to? A chimpanzee with a brain problem – the problem being that he didn't seem to have one. Not only that, but great chunks of his hairy coat appeared to be missing, which made him a brainless, semi-bald chimpanzee. Even so, I didn't forget my manners and decided I should introduce myself.

'I'm Dinah the Mynah,' I said, through gritted beak. How I hated that name!

The chimpanzee, who was still playing with his elbows, lowered his arms and looked across at me. I straightened on my perch, drawing myself up to my full height and trying to look

Calm and Elegant. Unfortunately, another bit of soot got up my beak and I sneezed. At least I managed to stay on my bit of twig.

'*Excusez-moi*,' I said, smoothing down my feathers.

'Ex-coo-what?'

'*Excusez-moi*,' I repeated. 'It's French. It means "excuse me".'

'Ah. French. I'm Arnold. Arnold Teabag.'

I began to tell him that I was not actually French myself, but he wasn't listening. He was holding his head on one side and pulling strange faces, pushing out his lips, puffing up his cheeks and then sucking them in.

'I've got this big lump in my mouth,' Arnold told me.

I sighed. I was beginning to feel like a nurse on Casualty Ward. 'Really?'

'Yes. I'll show you, look.' He opened his mouth and an enormous pink thing flopped out of his mouth.

'Is that it?' I asked.

'Yes.'

'That's your tongue.'

'Really? Is it dangerous?'

'Only if you don't think before you talk,' I hissed.

Arnold sat there, sticking his tongue in and out of his mouth. He pinched the end with his fingers and pulled it out as far as possible, before letting go so that it snapped back into his mouth.

'Ow!'

Then, just as I was beginning to think he couldn't possibly do anything more stupid, he slowly lifted one leg, leaned slightly to one side and made a long, rumbling noise from somewhere beneath that I shouldn't mention. He gazed across at me with enormous sadness.

'I have an air leak,' he explained. 'It keeps happening. I'm losing air all the time.'

Arnold shifted his body the other way and let off another little rumble. Then he started leaping upwards, jerking his head into the air and taking great gulps, as if he were trying to catch it.

'Got to get more air,' he cried, 'before it all leaks out.'

Well, I ask you: what would you have done? What would you have said? I reckoned the best thing to do would be to shoot him and put him out of his misery. Did I say this chimp was an idiot? I've changed my mind. Arnold was not just any idiot. He was THE World Record-Breaking Idiot of All Time.

And he'd come down my chimney. Lucky me.

I didn't bother to tell him that all that was wrong with him was a bit of wind. I thought it best to change the subject.

'So,' I began brightly. 'Where have you come from?' Arnold began to raise his arm, but before he could speak I hastily interrupted. 'Yes, I know you came down the chimney. And before that? Do you have a home somewhere?'

It was a simple question, but it had the most extraordinary result. Arnold dashed out of the fireplace, hurled himself beneath the coffee table and lay there, curled up in a tight ball of manky black hair, and he whimpered. His teeth chattered uncontrollably. His arms and hands were clasped tightly over his head.

I had never seen anything so desperately frightened in all my life. I moved to the end of my twig and stared down at this scared and shivering body beneath the coffee table.

'What's the matter? What's scaring you? It's OK. You're amongst friends here.'

I know, that last bit was stretching the truth a little, but only a very little. I mean, I didn't wish him any harm; I just thought he was an idiot, but his terror was beginning to scare me!

Slowly, Arnold began to unfold. He remained beneath the table, but he wouldn't look at me. He started to talk and the story he told sent shivers up my spine. It stirred up all kinds of memories of my own – memories I wanted to forget.

He was an escaped prisoner. He'd been held in a place he called The Dark House. There were hundreds of animals there – birds, beasts, reptiles – all prisoners. They were cramped so close together and fed so rarely that the house was full of disease and death. The place was run by a man and a woman. Food was often taken away as a punishment. The animals were beaten if they misbehaved. The man did the beating, but it was the woman who gave the orders.

I froze. It was as if an entire field of icebergs had floated on to my spine. This nightmare was so familiar. Was my past coming back to haunt me?

Arnold slowly lifted his face towards my cage

and looked straight at me. 'You must see The Dark House for yourself. I want you to come with me – now.'

This was all incredibly dramatic, but Arnold did rather spoil it at this stage by deciding to sit up straight. Since he was still under the coffee table, he ended up sitting there wearing the table on top of his head like some bizarre hat.

At that moment the door opened and Mark walked in and switched on the light.

6 Mark: The Midnight Visitor

I couldn't sleep. I opened my leopard eyes and gazed into the darkness. Leopards have brilliant night vision. They could spot a mouse at a hundred metres, in the pitch black. I narrowed my eyes, slipped out of bed and almost tripped over my own clothes on the floor. At least leopards don't have to bother about clothes. I pulled on my dressing gown and crept out to the landing. I sniffed the air, like a real leopard would. Everything was still, so I padded down to the kitchen.

I was going to make myself a drink and snaffle something to eat, but I heard strange noises coming from the front room. Dinah was muttering away like mad. At first I thought she was having a dream or something, but then I realized that something else was making a noise too, another animal. I know it sounds weird, but it almost sounded like they were talking to each other.

I pushed the door open and switched on the light. Dinah looked at me as if she'd just been caught red-handed doing something extremely naughty. And then I saw the chimpanzee!

There was a chimp sitting on the floor with our coffee table on his head. He was covered in soot and a big sooty trail led all the way from the fireplace to where he was sitting.

'Hello,' I said, like you do when you meet a chimp with a table on his head. Dinah and the chimp stared at me. He lifted one leg and . . . well, piffed, noisily. Dinah gave a small choking noise and slowly toppled backwards off her perch.

'Arrrk – dead,' she croaked, then promptly got up and began gabbling away, while the chimp looked at me with his immensely sad eyes.

I quietly moved across to the chimp, lifted the table from his head and sat down in front of him. 'I'm Mark,' I said, and I tapped my chest with one finger. 'Me Mark,' I repeated.

Dinah was fussing about in her cage, making a right nuisance of herself. I could see the chimp

was scared, so I patted my head and pointed to my spotted hair.

'It's OK,' I said softly. 'I'm not a real leopard. This is just for fun.' Then I thought that a chimp probably wouldn't think it was much fun to be a leopard anyway. Things were getting complicated. I just wanted him to understand that I wasn't going to harm him.

The chimp began tapping his own chest and then there was this really magic moment – he reached out and gently touched my chest! He did! It was like he was shaking hands or something. It was his way of saying 'hello'.

I tapped his chest and he tapped mine. I felt like I was almost talking to him. It was brilliant! Then he lifted one arm and made the bottom half swing from side to side. He chattered quietly, all the time he was doing this. He lifted his other arm and he made that swing from side to side too. I did the same. We sat there facing each other, making our arms swing back and forth. It was terrific!

The chimp lifted one leg and piffed, so I showed him how to cup a hand under his armpit and make a 'spluurrrgh!' noise. He began leaping up and down and howling. He obviously thought it was a pretty good trick, but he was getting a bit too noisy. I reckoned if I gave him some food, he'd calm down. He looked as if he needed feeding up anyway. Now that I'd had time to study him a bit more closely, I realized how thin and manky he was. His fur was all matted and big chunks were missing. I don't know if it had simply fallen out or if he'd been in a fight.

I got a banana from the fruit bowl and peeled it for him.

He stuck it in his ear.

Dinah thought all this was hysterical. She

screeched away, banging
her head on the floor
of her cage. She does
that sometimes. She's
a bit loopy.

I got another banana,
took a bite of it and
then handed it to the
chimp. This time he ate
it properly, although he did put the skin on top
of his head. It looked like a little yellow starfish.
Cute!

The chimp seemed to like me. He kept
reaching out and touching me, tugging at my
dressing gown, so I took it off and helped him
put it on. He thought that was great and lay on
his back kicking his legs in the air.

He slid across the floor and came and sat
right next to me, looking into my face. He
touched my chin and pinched my nose. He
pulled my ears. Then he climbed on my back.

He was all warm and hairy and tickly. I
couldn't stop laughing. I got up and we went
galloping round the room with the chimp
bouncing about on my back. Halfway round he

leaped off and when I turned to see where he'd gone he was swinging from the lampshade!

'Get down, you idiot!' I said. 'Get down before you break it.'

Then there was an awful scrunging noise and the whole light fitting came loose. It didn't actually break – it just came away from the ceiling and dangled down into the middle of the room. The chimp let go and went and sat on top of the TV instead.

I was beginning to think that this chimp was causing a bit too much trouble. I tried to get the light fitting back up, but even if I stood on a chair I wasn't tall enough. Besides, the chimp kept trying to climb up me, like King Kong on the Empire State Building.

I gave up and flopped on to the settee. The chimp came and lay there with his arms round me. I was exhausted. I don't know how long we were there, but I must have fallen asleep. I remember hearing Dinah and the chimp making quiet noises at each other, but it was the scrabbling from the fireplace that finally woke me up.

I opened my eyes and realized that Dinah's cage was wide open and there was no sign of her. Then there was more noise from the fireplace and I was just in time to see the chimpanzee disappear up the chimney, still wearing my dressing gown.

7 Dinah: The Dark House

Well! I'm brave, of course I am, but The Dark
House? Whoa! That was creepy. I don't like
creepy. I can look at spiders but that doesn't
mean I want to touch them. I can look at
worms, if they don't wriggle. But I don't like
creepy, and the idea of The Dark House sent
feather-rattling shivers right through me.

Mark had fallen asleep. He looked almost
angelic – very odd. But Arnold was going on
and on at me about The Dark House. It was
obvious he wasn't going to give up on trying to
get me to go there and see for myself.

He didn't seem to notice that I was getting the
heebie-jeebies. He had pulled up a chair and
now he stood on it and carefully opened my
cage. He reached in and pulled me out. Oh yes!
Pulled me out, just like that.

Have you ever been pulled out of your cage
by a chimpanzee? I don't suppose you have.

Well, some doctors think that our personalities are formed from the experiences we have. I had just been removed from my nice, safe home by a large flea-bitten chimpanzee that had fallen down the chimney, and that was a very strange experience indeed. If I seem at all odd to you in the rest of this story, then blame it on Arnold Teabag.

He held me out behind his back. 'Can you see where the leak is?'

'Arnold, of course I can't see. You're wearing Mark's dressing gown.

Besides, you do not have a leak. You suffer from wind. That is all. It's harmless, but often smelly. Polite people do not talk about such things.'

The chimpanzee hung his head. 'It's The Dark House. It makes us go crazy. We forget what the real world is like, and we start to imagine things.'

You know something? I came over all motherly. I actually began to soften towards Arnold. I mean, he was OK. So maybe he was weird at times, but he did have an excuse, and we were just about to go and visit it.

'Fly up the chimney,' said Arnold. 'I'll follow.'

I flew. There was not much else I could do, with a hulking chimpanzee following me. Arnold went skedaddling down a drainpipe and set off at a lope across the silent back gardens while I flitted from one tree to another.

'I'm losing my beauty sleep over this,' I told him, but he just kept on at a steady pace. I followed in silence until at length he came to a halt in a dank and gloomy garden, overgrown with weeds, brambles and the great, black, wet leaves of some monstrous plant that appeared to be invading everywhere.

'This is it,' Arnold announced, in a barely audible whisper.

Did I say I didn't like creepy stuff? The house I was looking at wasn't creepy. It was bone-meltingly terrifying. A smell of death and despair drifted from its walls. It was gaunt and gloomy. The windows were blank rectangles of darkness.

Ivy clawed the walls like a million tiny, green, scrabbling hands, plucking and pinching the bricks.

From inside came strange, haunting noises – howling and hissing, whining and whimpering, rustling and scratching and the sound of endless, secret digging.

'You hear the digging? That's Garbo. She's a lynx. Lovely creature, got sweet little tufts on her ears. She's digging a tunnel. It's her fifth one. She won't make it, but she doesn't give up hope. Everyone is desperate to escape.'

'But you *have* escaped,' I said. 'Why come back?' This was a good question. After all, I'd escaped too, but there was no way I wanted to go back.

Arnold looked at me. 'These animals are my friends. Not just the other chimps, but everyone. I want the whole lot released. Do you mind if I ask you something? When you close your eyes can you see anything?'

'No. Everything goes dark when I close my eyes. That's what is meant to happen.'

The chimpanzee gave a low sigh. 'I see things sometimes. I see trees. I see leaves and branches flashing past me. I see green. I think I'm going mad.'

'You're not going mad, Arnold,' I said softly. 'The things you're seeing are like dreams or memories. I think you are remembering your days in the forest.'

'Really?'

'Yes. It's a good thing to remember.'

'I'm not mad?'

I swallowed hard. I was going to say, well, yes, you are a bit mad actually, as chimps don't go around gulping air because they leak – and that's just for starters. But I didn't say that.

'You're not mad, Arnold.'

He smiled briefly and then stared at the house. 'Come on.' He quickly scaled the drainpipe and slipped down the chimney. I tried to ignore my thunderingly terrified heart and followed him into the stinking darkness.

I wasn't at all prepared for what I found, and I should have been. After all, Arnold had already warned me. Not only that, I had been there myself. I had lived there and suffered it.

The room was full of cramped, filthy cages. Chimps were crammed into some, monkeys into others. They huddled against each other, silently staring at Arnold and me. A faint fluttering made me look up and there, upon shelves going right round the room, were dozens of tiny cages full of birds. They hardly had room to stretch one wing, let alone two.

The nightmare had returned. I knew this place. Oh yes. This had once been *my* home, *my* prison. I was scared. I was angry. I was gagging on the stench of cages and animals that hadn't been cleaned out in months. Arnold put a finger to his lips and signalled me to keep quiet.

'Are there many more?' I whispered.

'Every room. The house is stuffed. They've all been smuggled in.'

My heart almost stopped beating. My captors were at it again, only this time on a far bigger scale.

'There are vampire bats upstairs, thousands of them, and vultures. In the kitchen there are snakes and lizards. South American frogs in the toilet, hyenas in the garden and a hippopotamus in the bath.'

'A hippopotamus!'

'Shhh! Don't squawk.'

'*Excusez-moi!* I do not squawk! I'm a ladyffffff . . .'

A long, hairy arm suddenly shot out as Arnold clamped his smelly hand over my face. It was too late. A woman's voice drifted down from above. This time I turned to stone. I knew that voice. Oh yes!

'Jaundice? Did you hear something? We'd better take a look. Get out of my way, you stupid oaf!'

'Sorry, Mistress Divine, sorry.'

Footsteps on the stairs – Arnold slipped back into the chimps' cage, made a zip motion across his mouth and pointed to the curtains. I flew up and hid. A moment later the door creaked open and the light was switched on.

It was her all right. She was one of the most beautiful women I have ever seen – tall and elegant, with short, spiky blonde hair that set off her high cheekbones. Her green eyes sparkled like jewels. She looked completely out of place in that hell hole. It was difficult to believe that she could have anything to do with such a sordid place. But I knew better. I had once been imprisoned by Divine.

Waiting behind her, as always, was her partner, Jaundice, the one who did the dirty work. Divine had the evil ideas but she made Jaundice carry them out. He was short and stocky. His head looked as if it had been hammered on to his shoulders with a pile driver. All that thumping and thudding had made his ears stick out and his nose stick in. He had bandy legs and long arms with massive hands on the ends, like the great clanking clawing buckets you get on road diggers.

So, the pair of them were now running an illegal animal racket. They made thousands of pounds by selling the sort of wild animals that couldn't be found in any pet shop, creatures that were in danger of extinction or too dangerous to be kept in ordinary homes. And while they were waiting to be bought, the animals were shackled in The Dark House. Disease had taken hold and was spreading rapidly.

Divine scanned the room carefully. 'Another dead monkey,' she hissed. 'Give the body to the hyenas to eat, Jaundice. If they don't stop dying, we shall have no animals left to sell. They need to be treated. I must put my plan into action at once. Come on, there's nothing going on here. Put out the light.'

The light went off and the door was shut. I flew down to the chimps' cage, trembling. 'Divine has a plan,' I whispered. 'Do you know what it is?'

Arnold shrugged. 'She wants to catch a vet. What kind of animal is a vet?'

'It's a kind of human.'

'Can you eat him?'

'No, Arnold, you can't. Don't you understand? Vets are people who look after animals. Divine wants to catch a vet who will cure all the animals here, so that she can sell them.'

Arnold cheered up considerably. 'That's good! We shall all get better!'

'Yes, you will get better, but it isn't good because you will still be prisoners and you will stay in cages for the rest of your lives. Heaven knows what she will do with the vet once she doesn't need him any more. She won't let him go in case he tells everyone what she's doing. I smell trouble and danger.'

Arnold lifted his head and sniffed noisily. 'I can only smell widdle and dung,' he said. 'What do trouble and danger smell like?'

I ignored him and gazed around the dreadful room. One by one the animals turned to look at me from behind bars. Their eyes pleaded silently. 'We've got to do something before it's too late.'

Arnold sidled across to me. 'I already have a plan.'

Amazing! Arnold the Chimp Chump Champion had a plan! Maybe he wasn't such a nincompoop after all. My hopes began to rise. Together we would do this thing! Together we would release all the animals, overpower Jaundice and Divine and destroy The Dark House forever.

'You have a plan? What is it?'

'You and I are going to stop her,' he announced, just as if he was suggesting we went shopping.

'That's it? That's the whole plan?'

Arnold flashed a pleased smile at me. 'Yes! Simple plans are always best,' he said. 'I can see you're impressed.' He lifted his leg. '*Excusez-moi*,' he murmured, 'as I believe you Frenchies say.' I held my beak.

My brain was racing. We had to do something, but what could a brain-dead chimp and a small mynah bird with a smattering of French manage against such evil villainy? And what was Divine's plan? I had a nasty, uncomfortable feeling that something terrible was about to happen.

8 Mark: Dad Falls in Love, I Think!

Dad woke me up. It took ages to realize where I was and then I had to work out how I'd got there. Dad stood there holding Tamsin while he waited for me to get the sleep out of my eyes and my brain.

'Interesting night?' he asked.

'What?'

'Was it a good party?'

I hadn't a clue what he was going on about. Dinah gave a little chirrup and suddenly everything clicked. Her cage – it had been empty! The door was still wide open, but she was back in there. There had been a chimpanzee – no, that bit must have been a dream. After all, the chimp had swung from the . . .

. . . Oh. It wasn't a dream. The light fitting was still dangling just above the floor. There was soot all over the place.

'I can explain,' I began, wondering if I could.

'I'm listening,' Dad said quietly.

'I couldn't sleep. I came downstairs and there was a chimpanzee in here.'

'Of course there was,' agreed Dad, and I sighed with relief.

'You believe me!'

'No, of course I don't, but do go on, Mark. It's such a good story, isn't it, Tam?'

'There was a chimpanzee. It went up the chimney. It was wearing my dressing gown.'

'Oh well, that should make it easy to spot. I'll ring the police and tell them to watch out for a chimp wearing a child's dressing gown.'

'Dad!'

'Mark! It's a bit far-fetched, isn't it?'

Dinah ruffled her feathers. 'Arnie!' she squawked.

'And what about this light? I suppose the chimp swung on it, did he?'

'Yes.'

'So you weren't being a chimp yourself, fooling around to discover what it was like to be a chimp?'

'No!' I tapped my hair angrily. 'I'm a leopard, Dad.'

Dad studied me in silence and then shrugged. 'OK, if that's your story, so be it. But if you think you're going to help me at the clinic this morning, then you're going to have to get this room spotless first of all. Understood?'

Tammy reached towards the light flex. 'Want to be a monkey, Daddy.'

Dad glared at me. 'See what you've started? Oh, and by the way, why is Dinah's door open?'

'I don't know.'

'There's a banana skin in her cage. Did you give her a banana last night?' I shook my head. 'OK, let's try to work this out. Dinah opens her cage, something she's never managed to do before. She flies out, grabs a banana that's too big for her to carry by herself and takes it to her cage. She peels it, no doubt using her incredibly useful and clever wings, eats it and throws the skin to the floor of her cage because we haven't been thoughtful enough to provide her with a litter bin.' Dad beamed at me. 'Is that what happened?'

'It was the chimpanzee,' I grumbled. 'He put the first one in his ear.'

'Oh, Mark, please!'

'He did, Dad. He put it in his ear.'

'Mark, chimps are intelligent animals. They don't put bananas in their ears.'

Obviously, there was no point in trying to convince Dad, so I spent the first part of the morning sorting out the front room. I had to leave the light for Dad. It was almost half past ten before I could go across to the surgery and by that time things were pretty busy. I like it when it's like that because I can learn loads more things about treating animals.

Dad usually explains what he's doing as he goes along, but this morning Dinah wouldn't stop interrupting. She was making such a fuss and throwing herself against the bars of her cage. It might have been because we had a snake in the surgery, although she's never been

scared of snakes before, and this one was pretty
small.

It had been brought in by some amazingly
beautiful woman. She was tall and elegant, with
her hair cut very short and a bit spiky. Maybe
that sounds ugly, but it suited her. The moment
she entered, the room filled with her scent. It
was like a meadow in full flower, fresh and light
and lovely.

Dad definitely thought she was Wonder
Woman! He couldn't take his eyes off her. My
heart was starting to pound and I was
wondering if maybe, maybe, maybe this was the
woman for him! Could it be? He was certainly
taken with her, and she seemed pretty friendly
towards him.

Dinah was screeching so loudly you'd think
she was being swallowed by a crocodile. She
flapped about, banging against the sides and
rattling her beak across the bars. She kept
screeching something at us. It sounded like
'darkuss' or something.

'Your bird's very noisy,' said the beautiful lady.

'It might be your perfume, or perhaps the
snake is scaring her,' Dad answered. 'Mark, put

the cover over her, will you? This is my son. He usually helps out on Saturday.'

'Pleased to meet you, Mark. Interesting hairstyle, and I can see you get your good looks from your father.'

Wow! I shot a glance at Dad. He was crimson! Come to that, I could feel myself blushing too. Dad frowned and fiddled with the box the woman had brought.

'Let's take a look at this snake. It's quite a rarity. I don't often see one like this.'

'No? It was my husband's snake.'

I groaned inwardly. Of course, she was bound to be married. Dad had picked up on this too.

'Oh, so you're married then, Mrs . . .?'

'Please, call me Divine. All my friends call me Divine.'

'Divine? What a beautiful name,' beamed Dad. He did like her! I knew it! 'A beautiful name for a beautiful lady.'

Double wow! I couldn't believe what I was hearing. I kept absolutely still in the corner of the room. I didn't want to break the magic of this moment. There they were, looking deep into each other's eyes, with great, big, silly smiles

right across their faces. Divine gave a little
sigh.

'I *was* married. My husband died, poor man.
He was bitten.'

'I'm sorry. Was it a snake?'

'No. A hippopotamus.'

'A hippopotamus! How horrible for you!'

'It was worse for Boris,' said Divine. 'Yes.
There was lots of blood. Boris was a big man,
but I never guessed he had so much blood in
him and it all came out, you know. The thing
about hippos – you don't mind me telling you,
do you?' Divine broke off and touched Dad's
fingers. Dad was looking very concerned and he
began gently patting Divine's hand.

'No, do go on, if it helps.'

'Oh, it does. You see, the thing about hippos is
that they have very big, very strong teeth, but they
are rather blunt. Poor Boris – he wasn't exactly
bitten to death – he was more, sort of *mashed*.'

'Urgh!'

'Yes, and here's an odd thing: the hippo was
caught the very next day and when they opened
up the beast's belly do you know what they
found?'

Dad and I stared at her, hanging on her every word.

'All that was left was one sock, one blue sock,' she said, quietly shaking her head. 'With a diamond pattern on it. I'd given him that pair of socks for Christmas only a few weeks earlier . . .' Poor Divine began to sob. Dad put a comforting arm round her shoulder and handed her a tissue.

There was a very loud screech from beneath the cage cover. 'Darkuss! Darkuss!'

'Shut up, Dinah!' I hissed.

DARKUSS! DARKUSS!

'Unusual bird,' observed Divine between sniffs, gazing curiously at Dinah's cage.

'Everything is unusual around here these

days,' Dad said evenly. 'One never knows what's going to happen. I wouldn't be surprised to find a chimp in my front room, or even an elephant.'

Divine smiled at me. She had the most amazing smile. It was like a fabulous sunrise.

'Your wife must be very proud of you,' she said.

'My ex-wife lives in America,' Dad answered, with a little scowl.

'I see, so she's slipped away and left you with the problem of working and looking after Mark.'

'And Tamsin. She's four. It's not easy.' Dad sighed. 'The childminder refuses to look after Tammy any longer and she doesn't start school for two months. It's a bit of a headache, to tell you the truth.'

Divine raised her eyebrows. 'Oh dear. That must be difficult.'

'It is. Still, let's sort out this snake.' Dad examined the creature for about the fifth time. Every time he started he seemed to end up gazing at Divine instead. I was finding it very hard to keep my enormous grin inside my mouth instead of outside. I was so happy. Dad definitely liked her!

'Mr Draper . . .'

'Please, call me Peter.'

'Thank you. Peter, I have an idea. I do hope you won't mind my suggesting this. Why don't you let me look after your daughter? I don't work at the moment. I have looked after children before. I could even look after her at your house, so that you are close by.'

There was an explosion of noise from under Dinah's cover. It sounded as if a brass band had just erupted inside it, and Dinah was screaming and screaming, 'Darkuss! Darkuss!'

Divine stared at the cage as I banged the side with my hand until Dinah stopped.

'I couldn't possibly ask you to do something like that,' said Dad, while I kept my fingers crossed behind my back and thought, Please, please let Divine look after Tamsin. It will be brilliant!

'But you're not asking, I'm offering,' Divine pointed out. 'How about we try it for a week? Then you can decide if you want to keep me on. What about that?'

'Are you sure? I mean, when would you be able to start?'

'Monday. I have nothing better to do and I would love to look after Tamsin. I'm sure we shall get on well. I'm very good with children and animals.'

So that was that. Divine was coming to look after Tamsin and that meant that Dad would see even more of her and they were bound to fall in love because they obviously liked each other and everything was going to be utterly brilliant!

9 Dinah: Spot the Dog

Are they deaf? Are they totally brain-dead? I
tried to tell them, over and over again. I rattled
my bars. I banged my beak. I gave myself a
massive headache trying to get them to
understand. I thought humans were supposed to
be intelligent! I mean, there was Divine, right
under their noses! The very woman who had
almost killed me with a vacuum cleaner. *And* she
knew who I was. Oh yes! I'd seen the way she
looked at me.

I tried to tell them and what did they do?
Did they listen? Did they say, 'Ooh, dearie me,
Dinah says you're a nasty piece of work and we
mustn't listen to you'? What did they do? They
shut me up!

Oh yes! Very clever, I don't think. Humans,
eh? What do you do with them?

Anyhow, once they'd got the cover on I
thought I'd better sit there and listen. I might

learn something. I might find out what she was up to. And I did. She's going to start with Tammy. She'll get her claws on her and then she'll lure them over to The Dark House somehow, and that will be it – trap sprung!

Why couldn't they see what was right under their noses? All they saw was how gorgeous she was, how beautiful, and didn't she smell wonderful? Well no, actually, she didn't. She stank. She stank of dead and dying animals.

I was in such a state of shock by the time Divine left that Mark took my cover off to see if I'd died or something.

'What was all that noise about?' he asked. 'Why do you keep saying "darkuss"?'

'House,' I said, clearly and slowly, and I fixed him with one eye. 'Dark House.'

'You daft bird,' laughed Mark.

I was trying to save

DARK HOUSE

his life and he was laughing at me! He tried to tickle me under the chin, so I bit his finger. Ha ha. Mynah joke.

I was just thinking that humans were quite probably the most stupid invention ever, when the next patient came in and I immediately settled down for a bit of fun because guess who it was?

Miriana – the Madwoman from Romania! Remember her? She was back, and she'd brought a dog with her, a dog with spots. Mr Peter wasn't at all pleased.

'Good morning,' he said, ever so stiffly.

'Oh,' said the Madwoman. 'You are Mr Snappy this morning, I think. You have no smile?'

'I'm very busy,' said Mr Peter, even more stiffly. 'What have you brought today? Is it alive or dead?'

Miriana lifted the creature on to the examining table. 'Is dog – you no tell? You strange vet if you no tell dog. She verrry sick. You see. She has spots. I think it is, how you say, German missiles.'

Well! I fell off my perch laughing and Mark started sniggering in the corner.

'German measles,' corrected Mr Peter. 'Which is very surprising, because dogs don't get measles.'

He bent over the little terrier, closely examining the red spots, while Miriana waited. Mr Peter straightened his back and glared at her.

'These spots have been put on with lipstick,' he said coldly.

'SQUA$@*%ARFF!'

I'd only just climbed back on my perch and there I was on the floor of my cage again, spluttering with laughter, while Miriana gave Mr Peter a look of shocked surprise.

'No! Is lipstick? Where dog get lipstick? Why dog put on lipstick?' A good question, I thought. I mean, I know dogs are stupid, but I'd never heard of one wearing lipstick before.

'The dog didn't do it. You did it.'

'Me? You think I mad? I no do this. Dog do this. Dog verrry sick – has German missiles.'

'There is nothing wrong with this dog,' insisted Mr Peter.

'Oh yes, dog sick. How many dog you know wear lipstick? Dog must be mad. Dog need psychiatrist.'

'You're the one that needs the psychiatrist,' growled Mr Peter, wiping the little spots of lipstick off the dog's coat. 'Why do you insist on coming to my surgery with an animal that has nothing wrong with it?'

Miriana's eyes widened and she shook her head. 'You no understand? Men are so stupid.'

'Thank you,' Mr Peter said with an icy smile. 'That's the nicest thing anyone has ever said to me.'

Miriana burst out laughing. 'Is good joke! OK, I tell you why I come. Is because I like you. You man, I woman. We are good for each other, I think. I make you happy. Happy ever forever.'

'Oh, for heaven's sake stop saying that,' cried Mr Peter. 'This is not some fairy tale!'

'Why you angry?' asked Miriana quietly.

'Because, because you are utterly . . .

unbelievable!' yelled Mr Peter. 'And you're driving me mad. Take your spotty dog and go away!'

'Is not my dog,' said Miriana with a shrug.

'What do you mean, it's not your dog?' Mr Peter was utterly bewildered. Miriana gave another little shrug.

'I find outside. You ask for sick animal so I bring you sick animal.'

'Does it have a name?' asked the vet.

'Yes.'

'And it's called . . .?'

A third shrug. 'I don't know,' murmured Miriana, with an almost invisible smile.

'But you said it had a name!'

'Of course. Everyone know all dog have name, but I don't know what they are. Do you? You know name of every dog in world? You must be very clever man. Brain as big as space station, I think!'

Oh yes! This was getting better and better. I really liked this strange woman. There was something about her that made me feel there was a lot more to her than she was letting on.

Mr Peter tried to stay calm, but the effort just

made him look silly and pompous. 'Please take this dog back to where you found it. You cannot go around the streets picking up dogs and painting them with lipstick. Mark, it's time to take Tamsin back to the house. While you're at it, you can see this person out, and do make sure she actually goes.'

Miriana picked up the dog and made big eyes at Mr Peter. She pulled a long face. 'OK. I take. I go. Bye-bye, Mr Vetman. See you tomorrow.'

10 Mark: More Mad Stuff

I opened the door for Miriana and she marched back into the waiting room where she promptly handed the dog over to Julie, who got out a tissue and wiped off any remaining spots of lipstick.

'Thank you. She is good dog.'

'Yes, she belongs to Mr Cameron. He's on holiday for a week. He always leaves her with us when he goes away.'

'You won't say I put lipstick on his dog?'

Julie chuckled. 'He won't mind. He'll think it just as funny as I do. Anyway, have you won over Peter yet?'

I listened to all this with growing astonishment. Julie and the Madwoman seemed to be plotting together. This wasn't what I had planned at all. Things were getting too muddled for me. I'd only just sorted out Dad and Divine – they were getting on like a house on fire. Now Julie was encouraging Miriana.

'How did you get on?' Julie asked the Madwoman.

Miriana growled. 'Oh, he's like a bear, you know, grrrr.'

I couldn't help smiling. Miriana was about right. Dad *was* like a bear sometimes, all gruff and big and bristly.

Julie laughed. 'You should never give up, you know.'

'I not so sure. There are – how you say? – plenty more fish to fry.'

Julie laughed. 'You mean there are plenty more fish in the sea. I don't think you want to fry them.'

Miriana gave a tired smile. 'Maybe I want to fry some of them. My trouble – I have big trouble – is I *like* Vetman. I know he cross with me, but his eyes are kind. Only cross because he don't know what to do. He is good man with big heart.'

'Yes,' agreed Julie. 'He's a good man.'

There was a tremendous barking outside and an enormous Alsatian came flying through the door, dragging along a man on the other end of the lead.

'SIT – TWINKLE!' yelled the man, while the

dog roared and yowled and snapped at everything in sight, lashing out on the end of its lead, its jaws slavering. 'TWINKLE – SIT!'

The Alsatian carried on barking, barking, barking, until Tamsin was cowering behind Julie's counter and screaming with terror. Julie had turned completely white and was clutching Tammy to her knees. I climbed on to one of the seats, trying to keep my legs out of the dog's snapping jaws, and Twinkle barked so loudly I thought my eardrums would burst.

SIT-TWINKLE-SIT!!

Dad opened the surgery door to see what all the noise was about and had to slam it immediately as the Alsatian whisked round and made a tremendous lunge at him, all teeth and snarl and snapping jaws.

But Miriana simply stood there, stock still, and when the dog had his back to her she slipped down on one knee and laid a hand on the beast's back. She just said one thing. It wasn't a word, it was more of a sound: half grunt, half question – *Urh?*

Twinkle growled, but he slowly sank to the floor and lay down whilst Miriana continued to stroke the creature and murmur to him until he was still and quiet. At last she got to her feet.

'Poor thing,' she murmured. 'He was scared.'

Julie let out a long sigh of relief. 'Phew! We were all scared. It's OK, Tammy, the dog won't hurt you. Look, Miriana has told him to be quiet.'

And that was just about right. Miriana had told the dog to be quiet. *Told* him!

Dad's door opened again and he gazed down at the silent dog. It was as if nothing had happened. Twinkle was being as good as gold. Dad frowned at Miriana.

'Thank you,' he said, in his gruff Daddy Bear voice.

'You're welcome, Vetman,' she smiled.

'How did you do that?'

'Is old Romanian trick. My grandmother taught me. She is old Romanian.'

Tammy poked her head out from behind the counter. 'Bad dog,' she whispered. I went across and held her hand.

'I'll take Tam home, Dad.'

'And I will come with you and make sure she is all right,' said Miriana. We walked across to the house together. I was glad she was there. There was something I had to ask her.

'Do you like my dad?'

'No, is more than that. I am going to marry him.'

'Blimey! Does he know?'

Miriana gave me a kind of sideways glance. It was so funny, like she'd been caught doing something rude behind the teacher's back. 'I tell him, but he not listen. He is like man staring at pavement.'

'What?'

'You know, man walking along, he look at pavement, he don't look ahead so he no see what is coming. Your father, he no see me coming yet, but he will. He will.'

'How are you going to make him do that?'

'Oh, I make goo-goo eyes and tell him he so wonderful and he fall in love with me and we kiss and hug and kiss and hug. Then he say, "Oh, you are so beautiful, my darling, like star in sky. You are queen of my heart. Marry me at once!" Then everyone happy ever forever.'

Miriana made me laugh, but I was pretty sure things were not going to work out the way she wanted. 'I don't know,' I mumbled. 'You're very nice but I think he's got his eye on someone else.'

She stopped dead. 'There is someone else?'

'The new childminder. She's going to look after Tamsin. She's called Divine.'

'Divine? Pah! Is stupid name, like goddess. She is goddess? I don't think so!'

'She is very beautiful,' I ventured.

'Will she make a crockadipe?' Tamsin suddenly interrupted.

'I don't know, Tammy.'

'Will she make play dough?'

'I've no idea. You'll have to wait and see.'

'I can make play dough,' offered Miriana.

'Then *you* can come to my house and look after me!' Tammy cried.

'No, she can't,' I hissed at Tamsin. 'Stop interfering, will you? Dad's already asked Divine to look after you on Monday.' I tried to change the subject and asked Miriana how she had managed to calm the Alsatian.

'You children, so many questions!' Miriana shrugged. 'I always understand animals, ever since little girl. Is like I hear their thoughts and they hear mine.'

'Really? That's like me! I was talking with a chimpanzee last night – well, it felt like we were talking. He came down our chimney. Dad doesn't believe me, but he did.'

'That *is* very unusual, I think,' Miriana said.

'You don't believe me.'

Miriana shook her head. 'I believe you, Vetboy. I just say is unusual. Is no wonder your father finds it difficult. Where did this chimpanzee come from?'

'I don't know. He didn't look very well. And now he's got my dressing gown.'

The Madwoman was looking at me now with a strange expression. Her eyes were so dark and deep and she looked and looked at me, as if she was searching for something. 'Sometimes, at night, I feel there is something strange in this town. I think I hear animals howling. I open window and listen to darkness but there is nothing, nothing, just this feeling of big sadness somewhere, like dark cloud.' She shook her head. 'I sorry. Should not tell you this. Is not for children. I must go home. Bye-bye, Vetboy and Vetgirl!'

She is definitely weird. Really nice, but weird. Really, really nice. But definitely weird. I like her.

On the other hand there was Divine, who was truly beautiful and I was pretty sure Dad was head over heels in love with her. Bother. I turned to Tamsin.

'Who do you like best, Tam? Miriana or Divine?'

'Merry-ant,' she answered. She would.

11 Dinah: How to Make Play Dough

It's not fair. I was stuck behind the door, listening to that dog, and I hadn't a clue what was going on. Never mind, I was at home on Monday and Mark was at school so he didn't see what I saw then.

Monday started really badly. I couldn't believe that Mr Peter was going to let the Evil Mistress of The Dark House look after little Tam. It was like giving a newborn baby to a tyrannosaurus for safe-keeping. I tried to warn them but they treated me like I was some kind of starving idiot.

'Dinah's hungry,' said Mr Peter. 'Give her some breakfast.'

'Don't leave Tamsin with that monster!'

'Stop squawking, you daft twit. Have some cornflakes.'

'Daft twit yourself! I don't want cornflakes! She's from The Dark House! Don't let her in!'

But, of course, they did, because they're stupid, like most humans, except perhaps Mark. He's only half stupid.

Divine was dressed to kill. She arrived on the doorstep looking like some supermodel. You would have thought Mr Peter might have realized that she was not dressed like a childminder, but of course his eyes were on stalks.

'You go off to the clinic, Peter,' purred Divine. 'Tamsin and I will be fine.'

'What will you do? At Natasha's they do painting and singing and stuff.'

'Oh yes, we'll do all those,' said Divine.

The liar! The bare-faced liar! Well, I knew what she was up to, oh yes!

Peter grinned back like a lovesick schoolboy and went off to the clinic in his best mood ever. The door closed behind him and that left me, Tamsin and Divine in the house, all by ourselves. I was the only one who could save Tamsin now.

Did I say I was the only one? I was wrong. I am quite ready to admit it. I was wrong. There was one other person ready to save Tamsin from the Mistress of Evil. Want to know who it was?

Tamsin.

'We'll make some play dough,' she told the supermodel.

'I'm afraid I don't know how to make play dough.'

Well, that was no surprise to hear, was it?

'It's easy-peasy,' said Tammy. 'Daddy makes it all the time.'

'But I'm afraid I haven't made it, not ever.'

Tammy was astonished. So was I.

'You've *never* made play dough?' we chorused.

Divine shook her head and it was easy to see what she was thinking. Why did this wretched little child stare at her as if she was some stupid, gormless, brain-dead twit-head? (If Divine had looked at me she would have seen that I was staring at her like she was some stupid, brain-dead twit-head as well. I mean, even I know how to make play dough!)

But Tammy was not going to let Divine's lack of play-dough knowledge get the better of her. She got a big plastic bowl, pulled up a chair to the sink and stuck the bowl under the tap.

'We need water first,' Tammy declared. 'You

be the mummy and hold the bowl and I'll turn on the tap.'

Divine gritted her teeth and tried to smile cheerfully while Tam turned on the cold tap. *Ooh la la!* Water shot out, hit the bowl like the entire Niagara Falls thundering into a bucket, sprayed out in every direction and completely drenched Tamsin and Divine.

The supermodel screamed and dropped the bowl back into the sink, tipping its remaining contents down her own legs, filling her shoes and leaving her standing in an extremely large pool of very cold water, dripping and dropping, slipping and slopping. Ha ha ha! Served her right! Tamsin – one. Mistress of Hell – nil.

Tamsin, giggling hysterically, turned off the tap. 'You're wet!' she cried.

Divine wanted to strangle her. She wanted to feed Tamsin to a ravenous pack of wild beasts, quite possibly the hyenas in her own back garden. She wanted to put Tamsin on a rocket and send her to the furthest ends of the universe. But instead she summoned up all her will power and stayed calm. She needed to stay on the right side for the time being.

'Yes,' she said stiffly. 'I am a bit wet and you are too.'

Tammy lifted the bowl from the sink. There was a small amount of water left in the bottom. 'I think that should be enough,' said Tammy. 'We only need a little bit.'

'We only need a little bit,' repeated Divine. 'In that case it's a good thing the rest of it went over me, isn't it?'

Tamsin looked at Divine and laughed. 'You're funny,' she said.

Maybe not exactly the words I would have used to describe The Demon of Darkness, but it certainly put Divine in her place.

'Now we get some flour,' said Tam. She pulled the chair over to the cupboards and began to go through them. 'There it is.'

You can see what's coming, can't you? You know what's going to happen? I was already upside down, banging my head on the floor of my cage and squawking hysterically. I almost wet myself! But Divine, she had no idea and just stood beside Tammy, watching.

'Go on!' I yelled. 'Go on! Go for it, Tam!'

Tammy reached up to the top shelf. It was such a big stretch for a small girl, but she managed to pull the flour to the edge and guess what? Oh yes! The bag slipped from her fingers, toppled forwards, and landed on her head. The bag split open and flour billowed out, mostly over Tamsin, but a large cascade splattered right across Divine.

Then the bag hit the floor – POOFF!! – and the remaining flour exploded into the air, filling the kitchen with

an enormous white cloud. From somewhere deep inside it came the sounds of spluttering and coughing and the scraping of a chair. Finally, Tamsin and Divine staggered out through the doorway, looking like two phantoms.

This time even Tamsin was speechless. Drenched now with water and flour, Divine gazed back at the wrecked kitchen.

'Does your father always make play dough like this?' she asked.

Tamsin shook her head. 'I think you'd better tidy up,' she whispered.

Divine's jaw dropped. 'I'd better tidy up? What about you?'

'I'm not very good at it,' said Tamsin, very matter-of-factly. 'I can only do untidying. I expect I'll do tidying when I'm five.'

Oh, Tammy! I love you so much! You are the cleverest girl in the world. Tamsin – two; Mistress of Hell – still nil.

'Can't you stop that stupid bird from cackling?' yelled Divine. She was beginning to crack.

'You can't stop me,' I cawed. 'I know all about you. I know what you're up to!'

Divine suddenly came storming up to my cage and glared in at me. I'm sure the centres of her eyes were red, like the fires of Hell. 'Don't you worry, sunshine, your days are numbered. I know who you are! You pesky rat of a bird.'

Rat of a bird? What kind of daft insult is that? You can be a rat, you can be a bird, but how can you be a rat of a bird? It's like telling someone they're an elephant of an ostrich. Complete nonsense. I stuck my tongue out at her.

'Pig!' she yelled. So now I was a pig as well.

She stood there looking pretty scary, as if she wanted to eat me or something. Luckily, the front door bell rang at that moment. It was Julie, from the clinic, with bad news.

'There's an emergency at Mark's school,' she said. 'It's being evacuated. Peter said could you take Tammy to the school, collect Mark and he'll catch up with you later? He knows it's a lot to ask, but he's desperate.' Julie paused a moment, staring at them. 'You're a bit messy, aren't you?'

'Never mind that,' growled Divine, snatching up her bag and searching for her car keys. 'An emergency, eh? Well then, I'd better see what I can do to help.' She grabbed Tammy by the hand and almost dragged her to the front door. 'Come on!' she cried, her eyes glittering like a snake's. 'It's an emergency. We're going to save Mark and your daddy! Ha ha!'

All Julie did was raise her eyebrows slightly. I was beside myself. I ranted and raved. No! No, no, no, no! Don't let this happen! Don't let this woman go off with Tamsin. THIS IS A BAD MOVE!

I threw myself all over the place. I yelled and screeched until I was hoarse, while Divine gathered up Tamsin, followed Julie out of the house, and the door shut on me.

Silence. I closed my eyes. The nightmare was turning into a screaming night *terror*.

12 Mark: Trouble – Big Time

When I got to school on Monday morning Sanjeev was waiting by the gate, looking very excited.

'I've got a spider – it's huge. It's a tarantula and it's poisonous!'

'It can't be a tarantula. They don't live over here. Why did you bring it to school?'

'There's something wrong with it. It's got some kind of skin disease. Can you fix it? I put it in the classroom because everyone was pestering me for a look.'

I wasn't sure about this. I'd never seen Dad work on a spider before and I was fairly sure I wouldn't know what to do. However, I knew I'd have to take a look at the creature if only to shut Sanjeev up.

'It's pretty sick,' he muttered. 'Its skin has gone all weird. You'd better take a look.'

Very carefully, Sanjeev removed the lid of the

shoebox. Inside, huddled into one corner, was a very large, very hairy spider.

'Blimey!' I cried. 'It *is* a tarantula! But I can't see anything wrong with it.'

Sanjeev frowned. 'Last time I looked its skin was all funny, all sort of flaky.'

I straightened up and smiled. 'I bet there's nothing wrong with it at all. You just wanted to bring it in to scare us!'

'I never did!' cried Sanjeev. 'There was something wrong with it!'

'It's not moving much,' I admitted. 'Is it asleep?'

'Poke it with a pencil,' said Sanjeev. 'Then you'll see it move.'

I took a pencil and pushed at the spider. The body rocked forward and then settled back. I gave it a harder poke. This time the spider toppled right over. It lay on its back with its legs in the air.

'It's dead!' cried Sanjeev.

I looked at it more closely. Goose pimples began creeping over me, from my toes to the top of my head, until my scalp went all tingly.

'It's not dead,' I whispered. 'This isn't the

tarantula. It's the tarantula's skin. The real tarantula has escaped.'

Sanjeev stood there, open-mouthed. 'Spiders can't take their skin off!'

'They can. You know how snakes slough off their skin as they grow bigger, because their skin doesn't grow with them? Spiders do that too.'

'Never!' said Sanjeev.

'They do,' I insisted, and Sanjeev gazed forlornly at the perfect copy of a tarantula that was still lying on its back in the bottom of his shoebox.

'So where's the real tarantula?' he asked. 'It's poisonous. It can kill. What are we going to do?'

We stared at each other. It was like the ground had just vanished beneath my feet. My heart was thumping and my brain was in a whirl. I shut my eyes and crouched down on the floor.

'Why are you screwing up your face?' whined Sanjeev. 'What are you scuttling about the floor for?'

'Shhhh. I'm trying to think like an escaped tarantula.' I heard Sanjeev groan, but he kept quiet. I was asking myself, If I was a tarantula looking for a hiding place, where would I go? I got to my feet.

'I want every little nook and cranny searched from top to bottom. Take it bit by bit. You start over there. I'll take the big cupboard.'

'Won't it be dangerous?'

I shook my head. 'Tarantulas don't bite if you stay calm. Use a ruler or something like that to lift anything that the spider might hide under.'

'Supposing it jumps on me?' asked Sanjeev.

'It's not a leopard. Just take it easy. Don't be scared.'

'If you're not scared, why are you wearing Miss Pettigrew's scooter helmet and gloves?'

'It's a precaution,' I explained. 'I can't poke about in this cupboard with a ruler, can I? I shall have to use my hands.'

'You look stupid,' Sanjeev muttered.

'I'll look even more stupid dead, with a spider clamped to my throat, won't I?'

We began to go through the classroom. Soon there were great piles of books and stuff that we'd searched. I pulled everything out of the cupboard, shelf by shelf. There were mountains of PE shoes, leotards, shorts and even a pair of

underpants with a name label: *Sanjeev Mistry*. I
waved them at him.

'Hey, Sanjy – I've got your underpants!'

'Just exactly what is going on here?'

I froze. It was Miss Pettigrew *and* Mr Raza.

'Last week I came in here and you were
brandishing Miss Pettigrew's trousers in the air.
Today you've got Sanjeev Mistry's underpants.
Whatever is the matter with you, Mark?'

'Plus he's wearing my scooter helmet, and my

gloves,' frowned Miss Pettigrew. 'And look at the mess they've made!'

'It's the spider,' Sanjeev began to explain, but Mr Raza cut him dead.

'The spider? Don't be so stupid. You can't blame all this mess on a spider! Do you think I'm some kind of idiot?'

I had to get them to understand. 'It's a tarantula,' I cried.

Mr Raza folded his arms across his chest and looked at me pityingly. 'Mark, I know tarantulas are large, but even a tarantula couldn't create such a rubbish tip as this! What did it do – stand on the shelves and hurl books across the room?'

I pulled off the helmet and took a deep breath. 'Sanjeev brought a tarantula to school, but it escaped. We're pretty sure it's in this room somewhere and . . .'

'. . . you're hunting for it,' Miss Pettigrew concluded quickly.

'A tarantula?' squeaked Mr Raza, rising on to his toes before beginning a curious, reverse tiptoe towards the door. 'A *real* tarantula?' His voice sounded so different, like one of those squeaky balloon things.

'Leave the room,' ordered Miss Pettigrew. 'Sanjeev, catch up with Mr Raza and . . .'

'. . . But he's running across the playground, Miss Pettigrew.'

'I can see that, but he must ring the emergency services. They'll get someone out to deal with it. First thing is to make sure that everyone is safe. Mark, where do you think the best place for everyone would be?'

'Out in the open, on the playground. The tarantula will most likely want to hide somewhere dark. It doesn't like wide open spaces.'

'Good thinking,' she said. 'I agree.' She went straight to the wall and hit the fire alarm button.

And then everything went mad. Bells clanged, sirens wailed. Children and teachers began to pour on to the playground. It was chaos. I found myself in a line on the playground, along with the rest of the class. I gazed around at all the school buildings – the classrooms, the library, the canteen, the sports shed, the shrubbery, the wild garden, the pond area. That tarantula could be lurking absolutely anywhere.

It wasn't long before we heard the first wailing

sirens and then four fire engines turned up –
four! There were firemen everywhere. Miss
Pettigrew told the Chief Fire Officer that there
was a spider, but no fire.

'It's a tarantula,' she explained. The Chief
Fire Officer nodded.

'Tarantulas have a nasty bite. They can't kill
humans, but it's very unpleasant and I expect the
children are worried.'

'Not just the children,' murmured Miss
Pettigrew, wondering where Mr Raza had got to.

'Tarantulas aren't really our department,'
explained the CFO. 'My men can stay here for a
short while; it will reassure everyone. We usually
contact one of the local vets in an emergency like
this. I'll get on the radio right away.'

And that was how Dad arrived, followed
closely by Divine. He was so glad to see her and
I know it was sort of the wrong moment and
everything because there was a tarantula alert,
but it was great to see Dad getting on so well
with her. She obviously liked him if she was
prepared to go to all this trouble. It turned out
she had come to collect me from school.

'You look a bit of a mess,' grinned Dad.

'Play dough,' moaned Divine. 'Tammy and the play dough.'

'You still manage to look wonderful,' Dad told her, and she gave him a ravishing smile.

'Tammy's in the car with me now. Come on, Mark.'

'You don't mind leaving school early?' asked Dad. Some stupid question!

'Of course not.'

'I don't know how long this is going to take. It's best if Divine looks after you for the moment.'

'I'll take the children to my house,' Divine told him. 'It will be easier for me to look after them there.'

'Of course. I'll catch up with you when this is sorted. I must dash.'

'I'll collect my reward later,' hinted Divine, with that lovely smile of hers. SHE BLEW DAD A KISS!

I followed Divine across to her car. I could see Tammy sitting inside, looking upset. Divine opened the door and practically pushed me inside. At once I realized something was wrong.

'For goodness' sake, shut your sister up,'

snapped Divine. 'I'm sick of her snivelling.' Her voice sent shivers down my spine and I was on instant alert. I reached across and held Tammy's hand. She gripped my fingers so hard it almost hurt.

My brain was racing. What was going on? Why had Divine suddenly turned into some kind of monster? It was like she had flipped or something. I was pretty scared, but Dad had once told me that when you are dealing with an animal they can sense how scared you are. If you can stay calm they are less likely to attack – so I tried to stay calm. I had Tammy to look after, for a start. She gave a tiny sob, but I put an arm round her and hugged her and she stopped.

When the car finally pulled up we were in a part of town I didn't recognize. We were outside a really creepy-looking house. The windows were smeared with dirt and ivy. The rusty-brown paintwork was flaking from the door and porch. I thought I saw a rat scurry along a window sill. The whole building gave off a feeling of darkness and evil.

Divine wrenched the rear door open and jerked her head towards the house.

'Inside,' she snarled, in a voice you didn't argue with. I couldn't believe how much she'd changed. Her beauty had somehow become twisted and cruel.

Just as we reached the front door, a loud howl drifted from inside, quickly followed by the scrabble of many paws, digging, scratching, clawing.

'I want Daddy,' Tamsin choked.

Divine bent down and put her face close to Tamsin's. 'Don't you worry. Your daddy will be here soon enough and then everything will be happy, happy, happy! Look, here's Jaundice, come to make you feel at home.'

The front door swung open. A man like a gorilla stood there, grinning at us with a mouthful of broken teeth. Tammy and I reeled backwards, but whether that was because of Jaundice or because of the animal stench that came pouring out through the open door, I couldn't say.

'Have you got their room ready, Jaundice?' asked Divine, in an ever-so-sweet voice.

'Yes, ladyship.'

A second howl, much louder than the first,

came down the stairs. Tamsin clung to me.

'It's all right, Tammy,' I said, looking around. In the gloom I could make out several pairs of eyes staring at us from a pile of filth-strewn cages.

'Are those chimpanzees?'

Divine beamed at me. 'Such a little clever-clogs, aren't you? Yes, they're chimpanzees. We also have vultures and hyenas and vampire bats and spiders and poisonous frogs . . .'

'. . . And a hippopotamus in the bath,' added Jaundice.

'And a hippo in the bath,' repeated Divine. 'Big teeth,' she reminded me.

'But those animals aren't legal. Nobody is allowed to . . .' I shut up quickly. But it was too late.

Divine folded her arms. 'Too clever by half. If only Jaundice here had your brains, I could have made something of myself, but he has the intelligence of a slug. As it is, young man, I see that you could cause me a lot of trouble. I'm afraid that you and your little squawk-box of a sister will have to go to your room.'

'That's all right,' I said, as calmly as possible.

117

'We'll wait outside until Dad comes to pick us up.'

An excruciating shriek of laughter burst from Divine and immediately set every creature in the house gibbering. 'Oh no, no, no, no!' she cried. 'That won't do at all. You see, your father must come inside. *That's the whole point.* And once he's inside . . . GOT HIM!' Divine clapped her hands in my face. She suddenly lowered her voice and hissed, 'Jaundice! Take them to their room!'

Jaundice grabbed us and carried us through

into the back room. In the middle of the floor stood a filthy, empty cage. I stared at it in disbelief, but Jaundice propelled Tamsin inside. Then his hand was on my head, pushing me in. He shut the door and padlocked it.

'Sweet dreams,' he growled, and left, slamming the door behind him.

Tamsin cuddled up close to me.

'I don't like it here,' she whispered. 'And I want my teddy.'

'You'll have to pretend I'm your teddy,' I told her. 'Don't worry. Dad will be here soon, and then everything will be all right.'

But secretly I knew that it was going to get even worse.

13 Mark: The Great Escape

I tried to think of something, but for once I'd run out of ideas. I kept telling myself I had to be brave. I was thinking that Dad would be coming to collect us soon. He would certainly think of something and everything would be all right. I suppose I thought Dad would suddenly turn into a Kung Fu king, or come bashing through the doorway in a tank. I know it's stupid, but when you're in the sort of hopeless situation Tammy and I were in that's the kind of thing you wish for.

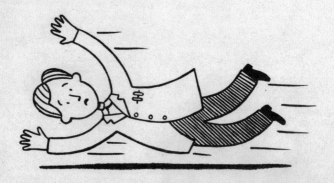

I heard Dad knocking at the front door. I heard low voices. Gradually, the noise level rose higher and higher. There was a lot of shouting and a bit of banging about. Finally, the door to our room crashed open and Dad came hurtling in and went sliding across the floor.

'Daddy!' cried Tamsin.

He struggled upright, but Jaundice wouldn't let him get to his feet. Divine was standing behind her slave, cackling like some evil old crone. I couldn't think why we once thought she was so beautiful.

'Are you two all right?' That was the first thing Dad said.

'We're OK. Are you?'

Dad managed a smile. 'I'm fine.' He glanced around the filthy room. 'I take it this is the best room in this de luxe hotel?'

'Of course,' answered Divine. 'I've put you in with the chimpanzees. I think it's best to keep things in the family, don't you?'

Dad ignored her and glanced across at Tammy and me. 'Looks like we've got a bit of a problem, Mark.' I nodded.

Divine burst out laughing again. 'A bit of a problem? No, no, no. There's no problem, my dearest, darling Peter. All you have to do is look after my animals. I want you to make them better, because if you don't, then your children will end up in an even worse state than they are at present. Do you understand?'

'You're a nightmare,' growled Dad angrily.

'Oh, Peter! You have upset me! Only this morning you thought I was a dream come true and now, oh dear, suddenly I'm a nightmare.'

She looked so victorious, so pleased with herself. It was hard to believe that we had once thought she was the most wonderful thing to happen to us.

'You're probably wondering why I picked you, dear Peter. Well, I'll tell you. I needed a vet. But how was I to choose one? And then – bingo! There it was in the newspaper: your darling little advert. It was so, so sweet. My heart bled for you, Mr Poor-Little-Lonely-Heart.'

Oh no, not that! This was all my fault! I couldn't look at Dad's face. I just stared at the floor. I wanted it to swallow me whole. I wanted to disappear forever and ever.

Divine affected an enormous sigh. 'Poor Peter. You came looking for a House of Love and what you found was a House of Horror.' The mock concern turned into a snarl as she bent over Dad and almost spat at him. 'If the animals get worse, your children get worse. It's as simple as that.'

Dad nodded. 'I get the picture, but if I'm going to treat these wretched creatures, I shall need my medicines and they are at the clinic.'

'Nice try,' crooned Divine. 'But you will have to do better than that. You're a vet. Vets always travel with a medical kit in their car. Isn't that so?'

Dad glared back at her, silent.

'I shall take your silence as a "yes". Hand over

your car keys and Jaundice will bring the medicine to you.'

Dad practically threw the keys at her.

'Thank you so much. The more you cooperate, the easier it will be for Mark and Tamsin.'

'What is it with you?' Dad demanded. 'Why are you like this? Why do you treat animals like dirt?'

Divine folded her arms across her chest. 'Like dirt? But I love animals, my darling Peter, I always have. I was going to be a vet, just like you, but no matter what I did, the animals seemed to die. I failed my exams because of them. If it hadn't been for the animals dying all over the place I would have passed! So now I do the next best thing and I look after them in my little house here.'

'And they're still dying all around you!' Dad pointed out.

Divine rushed forward and began kicking the chimps' cage, screaming at Dad. 'Shut up! Shut up! Shut up! Shut up!'

Now she was hammering on the top of the cage with her fists, her face twisted with rage. The chimps cowered inside, with their arms over their heads, and howled.

It was horrible. I don't know how long it would have gone on, but Jaundice came hurrying back into the room with the medical box from the car. He pulled her away from the cage.

'Mistress, don't upset yourself now. I have the medicine. You're overtired. You work too hard. Go and lie down. I shall make sure the animals get treated.'

Divine looked like some evil witch out of a cartoon film. She was all hunched up and white-knuckled, with her hair sticking out all over the place. She threw Dad such a red-hot scowl I thought he'd burst into flames on the spot, but she went.

Dad had no choice but to set about attending to some of the animals. He looked at the sickest ones first. It took ages. Many of them were too bad to be treated and he had to put several animals to sleep. At last Jaundice allowed him back. Dad was locked into a cage on his own, on the far side of the room. We could only stare at each other through the bars. Jaundice left us to it.

Dad looked completely haunted by the

horrors he had seen in the other cages. He kept muttering to himself, 'I've never seen such appalling conditions. I must do something.'

'I'm hungry,' wailed Tamsin.

Dad fished in his pocket and found the remains of a chocolate bar. He threw it across to us, but it landed on the floor, short of the cage. Now none of us could reach it. Tammy started to cry.

'I can't get it, Tam. I'm sorry. You'll have to suck your thumb.'

The chimps in the cages around us were fascinated by the remains of the chocolate. Maybe it was the silver wrapping paper, but they kept trying to reach out to it. They rattled their cages, clicking and clucking their tongues and lips, as if they were talking to one another.

Dad was examining his cage too, going over every little bit to see if there was a weakness somewhere, some way of getting out. It was hopeless. He settled back against the bars and looked across at me.

'Miss Pettigrew tells me you want to be a vet when you grow up.'

'Yes, but I –'

'When I grow up I'm going to be a crockadipe,' Tammy interrupted, her thumb half in, half out. 'I shall be a big, big crockadipe with lots of teeth and I shall get Divine and I shall go *Snap! Snap!* And I'll bite off her legs and *Snap! Snap!* I shall bite off her arms and then a really, really, really big *SNAP!* And I'll bite off her head and all her blood will come out and her brains and that will be the end of her!'

'I think we'd all like to do that,' said Dad, and he turned back to me. 'There's still lots to learn, Mark.'

'I already know loads,' I said proudly.

'That's true, but there's always more. It's important to know what kind of creature you are dealing with. Spiders, for example. Can you tell the difference between a big house spider and a poisonous tarantula?'

I was about to shout, 'Easy!' and then I thought, Hang on, why is Dad bringing this up? The penny dropped and I slumped back against the bars.

'It was a house spider?'

'It was pretty big,' Dad nodded, 'but a house spider nevertheless, and definitely not a tarantula.'

'Sorry.'

Dad smiled. 'Got you there! It doesn't matter. I thought it was quite funny, especially when I went to tell Mr Raza and found him standing on a chair in the dining hall. He said he was changing a light bulb. He was obviously convinced it was deadly poisonous!'

I knew Dad was trying to cheer me up, but I couldn't laugh. He asked me if I'd tried to get out of my cage, so I began another search, but stopped almost immediately. Something else had caught my eye – or rather, something *hadn't* caught my eye. The chocolate was no longer there. I looked all around. In a dark corner of the room a chimpanzee was sitting, examining the chocolate. And the chimp was wearing my dressing gown. I hissed at Dad and pointed.

'Which cage has it come from?' Dad asked. 'It's wearing a dressing gown just like . . .' His voice broke off as he twigged. 'Is that . . .?'

'It's the chimp that came down our chimney, Dad. Got you there! This must be where he came from. Look, he's out of his cage. Hey, hey, boy! Over here. Remember me?'

The chimp gazed across at me. He leaned to

one side, made an unpleasant noise and shuffled closer. I reached through the bars and tapped his chest. The chimp grabbed my hand. It didn't hurt – he wasn't squeezing or anything, just holding it. He put my hand on top of his head. Then he put it over his ear. And then over his mouth. At last he let me have my hand back, and he sat there, waiting.

'What's he doing?' asked Dad. 'Is he mad?'

I smiled excitedly. 'He's remembering the banana I gave him when he came to our house. I think he'd like another one.' I leaned towards the chimp. 'Sorry, old friend. I haven't got any bananas today.'

The chimp pushed out his lips, blew the most

enormous kiss at me, stuck his hand under one armpit and began pumping out a great symphony of raspberries.

Spplllurrgh! Spplllurrgh! Spllurrrgh! Spllurrrgh!

'Good heavens, he's gone mad,' muttered Dad. 'He's stark raving bonkers.'

'Dad! That's what I taught him. I showed him how to do that. He's so clever! He's remembered everything.'

I was so excited. Maybe, just maybe, this strange creature could help. I watched him move back to the others and he began chattering quietly with them. It was as if they were having some kind of discussion. All of a sudden, the one in the dressing gown began gibbering away excitedly. He rushed to the fireplace and vanished up it, only to reappear a moment later. He raced across to my cage, banged it, rushed back to the fireplace and vanished again. Once more he came back.

Dad was astonished. 'He's showing us the way out. He's showing us how to escape! If only we could . . . wait . . . I know! A message – we'll send a message!'

Dad pulled a scrap of paper from his pocket

and began writing furiously. 'I'm putting the address of this house and a note to say what's happening.' He carefully folded the message and pushed it through the bars of his cage. The chimp stuffed the note into his mouth and began to chew.

'No!' I whispered. 'Don't eat. Important message. You take.'

The chimp took the note from his mouth and gazed steadily at me, almost as if he was reading my thoughts. I pointed to the little fireplace in the room. 'Take the note,' I said slowly. 'Now go. Take the message and go!'

The chimp stood beside the fireplace. He stared back at us. All at once, he turned and came running back to my cage. He put one hand under his armpit and gave one final, glorious *sppplllllurrgh!* before scampering back to the chimney and disappearing. For a few seconds we heard the sound of him scrambling higher and higher and then there was quiet.

'As soon as that chimp is spotted he'll be caught,' muttered Dad. 'And whoever catches him will find the note – I hope. Keep your fingers crossed.'

'Daddy?' Tamsin asked sleepily. 'Will the chimp bring my chocolate back?'

Dad winked at me. 'Of course he will,' he said. 'He is going to bring back the Army, the Navy, the Air Force, the Police, the Fire Brigade, the Animal Rescue people, the Scouts and Guides and Cubs and Brownies, AND your chocolate.'

'Good,' said Tammy. She stuck her thumb in her mouth, closed her eyes, leaned back against me and fell asleep.

I wished I could sleep. I wanted to. I was so tired, but I had to stay awake. I had Tammy to look after and I needed to be ready, just in case. The room grew darker and darker. I heard Dad whisper it was almost midnight.

Midnight, and no rescue party. My heart grew cold. I could feel tears stinging behind my eyes. I blinked. I shut them hard. I told myself I would not cry, but they squeezed out by themselves.

14 Dinah: Mynah Bird
to the Rescue!

I'd been on my own for hours with no idea of
what was happening. I could hardly contain
myself. Somewhere in the town there was a big
drama going on. The telephone rang from time
to time, but the house was empty. I began to
wish that Mr Peter had taught me how to answer
the phone instead of French.

The hours ticked away and night came.
Where were Mr Peter and Mark? What was
happening to Tamsin? I sat and fretted. A
feather fell out. Another feather fell out. I was
going bald with stress!

All of a sudden there was a very noisy
scrabbling from the chimney, a cloud of soot
billowed out and Arnold crashed down into the
fireplace with a bone-jarring thud. He gave me a
glum look.

'I've lost my legs. They've fallen off.'

'You're sitting on them. They're under your backside.'

'Really?'

I didn't have any time to waste on this nonsense. 'Arnold, listen, there's big trouble. Divine has got Tammy.'

'She has Mark and Mr Peter too. They're all in cages at The Dark House.'

This just about floored me. What on earth were we to do now?

'I've got something for you,' said Arnold. 'The Mister man gave it to me, but you mustn't eat it.'

'Mr Peter? Show me.'

Arnold looked in his armpits. He looked in his leg-pits. He opened his mouth and felt around inside with his long, hairy fingers. Then he began poking at his ears. This was getting wearisome.

'Arnold, try looking in your pockets.'

He gazed at me with astonishment. 'I don't have pockets. Do you? Birds have *pockets*? I'd really like some of those, Dinah.'

Ah yes. I had forgotten that Arnold was terminally stupid. 'The pockets are on the dressing gown that Mark gave you. Look in there.'

He looked. He found the paper. Hallelujah! I looked at the scribbled note. 'It's a message. I bet Mr Peter wrote this.'

'He did. What does it say?'

'I don't know. I can't read. But it probably says "help!" amongst other things. That's what I would put on a message if I was stuck in a cage in The Dark House.'

'What are we going to do?'

'First of all, you can get me out of this cage. Then we'll take the message and give it to someone.'

'Who?' Arnold was fiddling with the cage.

'I don't know. I'll think about it. Come on.'

I whizzed across to the chimney and we both escaped on to the roof. I gazed out across the silent town and all of a sudden I realized how difficult my task was. How was I supposed to choose somebody? Suppose I gave the message to another animal smuggler by mistake? Suppose I gave it to someone too busy to help or someone who simply didn't care?

Arnold leaned over to one side. 'I've still got that leak,' he said. 'Are you sure I won't run out of air?'

'You'll be fine. Wait here. I'm going to try and find someone to give the message to. I can fly across town and see things more easily than you. If I spot someone, I'll come back and get you.'

I launched myself into the air and began my search. There were one or two people wandering the streets, but it didn't seem right to disturb them. I began to wonder what they would do if I appeared on their shoulder waving a crumpled bit of paper at them. Maybe they would think I was mad, shoo me away.

I kept flying, round and round, swooping over the houses. In the distance there was a kind of faint singing going on. It sounded so eerie and beautiful. I was almost pulled towards it. Where was it coming from? There was a light at a window, and a figure sitting there. Someone was singing a song of such sweetness, not a human song at all, an animal's song. It was an animal's song, sung by a human. What kind of human would do that?

I flew closer. I perched in a tree as close as I dared and I stared at the shadowy figure at the window. It was Miriana, the Madwoman from Romania!

In an instant I was off again, back to Arnold. 'I've found someone. She'll help us, I'm sure. She's mad – you'll like her. Come on, it's not far!'

Arnold began to make his way across the gardens. He was ever so grumpy about it. His dressing gown kept getting caught on rose bushes and twigs and stuff. By the time we reached Miriana's house it was torn and tatty, but at least we were there. Miriana was still at the window, singing.

'I haven't heard that song for ages,' murmured Arnold, his eyes glistening.

'The old ones are always the best. Let's go up.'

I was disappointed. I was expecting Miriana to be surprised. I flew straight to the window sill and landed with a flurry. 'Ta ra!'

She didn't bat an eyelid! 'I thought you might come,' she said. 'When there's trouble I always get unusual visitors.' A few seconds later Arnold hauled himself up on to the ledge.

Miriana reached out and touched Arnold. 'You are in bad way, my friend, but is no problem. We clean you up. This dressing gown is Mark's, I think. He give it you.'

'Mark!' I cried.

'Clever bird,' smiled Miriana. This was a truly intelligent woman. I mean, she could obviously see how bright I was. Oh yes!

'So, what is going on, eh? What's this? Some paper? Is message, yes?'

Ten seconds later she was on the telephone to the police.

A minute after that she was hurrying out of the house. She stopped at the door. 'Are you two coming?'

Did she really need to ask? I only hesitated for a split second. I knew it meant going back to The Dark House, to face my nightmares again, but now there was so much at stake. Mr Peter had once saved my life. It was time to return the favour.

15 Mark: Rescue!

The Invasion was swift and hugely noisy. The entire street must have been woken by the sound of the front door of The Dark House being broken down by four policemen with a battering ram.

The house shook with noise. The policemen were roaring at each other. The animals were howling and gibbering. Jaundice was bellowing at Divine and she was screaming back at him. I clutched Tammy close to me.

The police came swarming through the house, flashing torches and waving truncheons as they charged about. They soon found us and had the cages open in no time.

'Keep out of the way while we search the place,' ordered their chief. 'These animals are dangerous. OK, men, get up those stairs! Search the bathroom!'

'Urgh! There's a hippo sitting in the bath. It looks just like my granny!'

'This room is full of snakes and lizards. It's horrible. Aargh – spiders! I hate spiders! Gerroff, gerroff, gerroff! I'm going back.' A trembling constable tried to take shelter in our room, but his boss barred the door.

'Just keep searching, sunshine,' he ordered. 'Find those criminals.'

Jaundice made a break for freedom by plunging down the stairs in his pyjamas, straight into another five policemen, who were rushing up towards him. They met in the middle and the whole bundle of them turned into a kind of rolling, human snowball, made up of flailing arms and legs. The ball came tumbling down the steps, one by one, bumpety-bump, until it reached the bottom, where it broke into bruised bits.

Jaundice was carried out to the waiting police van. Meanwhile, the police rushed the stairs again, in a bid to capture Divine.

The first thing she did was release all the vampire bats, driving them from their room, so that an immense cloud of flappy, squeaky creatures surrounded the men on the stairs. The police tried to protect themselves by hitting out at the bats, but more often than not they hit each

other instead and soon they were rolling back
down the stairs for the second time.

In the
meantime,
Divine was racing
around the top of the
house releasing as many
animals as she could,
including the pygmy hippo,
which now stood at the top of the stairs looking
down at the police in complete bewilderment
and barring the way to anyone coming *up* the
stairs.

Dad had joined in the pursuit. I think he
wanted to get his hands on Divine and now he

pushed his way to the front and gazed up at the hippo.

'Let me go up,' he told the police. 'I know how to handle hippos.'

Dad was so brave! I knew he had put medicine down a lion's throat, but I had no idea he was good with hippos.

He grabbed a truncheon, made his way up the stairs and there was the hippo, staring right at him. It might have been called a pygmy hippo, but it looked gigantic to me.

'Come on, move, you big, fat lump,' ordered Dad, and he gave the beast a poke.

It might have been the poke that did it. It might have been that the hippo didn't like being called a big, fat lump. It might have been that just as Dad poked the creature a vulture swooped low overhead and said, 'Krarrrrkkkk!' (Which probably meant 'Make a run for it before they turn you into hippo pie!' in vulture language.)

Whatever, the hippo decided that it didn't like being upstairs any longer and it wanted to be downstairs instead. Dad was in the way. The hippo didn't bother with any 'excuse me', it

KRARRRRKKKK!

simply barged into him, knocking him backwards. Dad fell awkwardly, trapping his leg in the banisters. The hippo brushed him to one side and stomped off down the stairs.

Dad was helpless. His leg was in a bad way. One of the beast's massive toenails had sliced a gash in his forehead and blood was pouring out. The police went up to rescue him and I caught a glimpse of Divine as she looked back at Dad, a twisted smile on her face.

'Oh, Peter,' she teased. 'You look so

wonderful. Will you marry me?' Her cackling laugh was worse than all the vultures put together. She blew him a kiss and then she was gone. She had escaped.

Dad was taken straight to an ambulance. Tamsin and I sat inside with him and listened to the uproar from the house. Then the engine started up and we were heading for the hospital. It was only then I realized that my heart had been thundering away all that time, thumping and banging like a kangaroo in a box.

I didn't know what to do, what to think. I wanted to get to the hospital, so that Dad could be fixed up. I wanted to get to The Dark House, so that I could help the animals. I wanted to track down Divine, like a leopard closing in on his prey.

And then what? I had no idea what I wanted to do to Divine. I was absolutely furious with myself. I had been so stupid! This whole thing had been my fault. And all along I thought that Divine was the one, that she was the one who would be good for Dad and good for all of us. I stared out through the window of the racing ambulance in silence.

16 Dinah: The Marvellous Madwoman

Such a noise! The street was full of people when we arrived. Miriana wanted to go in, but there were police at the door. She looked at the police cars outside and saw Jaundice sitting in one of them, scowling at everything. But there was no sign of Divine.

Miriana pulled Arnold away from the door. 'Come, my friend, we go from here. Is too much noise, too much rushing. Divine Goddess will be trying to escape. I must think.'

She lifted Arnold on to her back and carried him up the road, while I perched on her head.

She didn't seem to mind and her hair made a wonderfully soft nest. When we got to the corner of the street she stopped.

'OK. Now, you stay quiet and I listen.'

There was a short silence. Arnold began leaning to one side.

'Arnold – shhhh! Not now!' I hissed.

'But I'll explode,' he warned.

'Just keep quiet!'

There was a long silence. Miriana closed her eyes and listened. I closed my eyes and listened, trying to catch the faintest sounds of Divine making her break for freedom. Then we heard it.

Spppllrrrrrgh!

'Arnold!'

'Sorry.'

'Stay here,' murmured Miriana. 'Is danger on street. Leave to me.'

At that moment Divine appeared from behind a hedge. She came running across the road, quite unaware of us, and immediately behind her came the hyenas, the whole pack, snarling and slavering. She was using them as guard dogs!

Miriana got up from beside us and stepped right in front of her.

'Hello, Goddess,'
she growled.

'What do you want?
Get out of my way!'

'Oh, so sorry. You
want go somewhere?
But no, you must
stay.' Miriana

scowled. 'You bad girl. You stand in corner!'

'Out of my way or I shall set my dogs on you!'

Miriana gazed at the growling beasts. 'You
think these dog? You not so clever. Is hyena.
Very nasty bite.'

Divine was not going to waste any more time
and she turned to the snapping monsters. 'Get
her!' she cried.

The beasts leaped forward, but Miriana
hardly moved. She held out one hand, stared
straight at the scavengers and she purred.
Unbelievable! I've seen some neat stunts, but this
was incredible! Miriana stood there and simply
purred in her low, rolling voice.

'Oh, you nice animals, so soft, so handsome. I
like you, oh yes, like little babies. Yes, you roll
over and I tickle your tummy like so.'

Divine wanted to scream. The hyenas were backing off. They sat down in the road. They lay down. Two of them rolled over and Miriana gently scratched their bellies. Miriana looked up at Divine. 'This very dangerous animal,' she smiled.

At which point Divine completely lost her cool and lashed out with a flying kick. Miriana caught the foot with one vice-like hand. For a second the two women glared at each other, eyeball to eyeball. Miriana let go, but still they stared at each other.

'Now, you all come with me,' Miriana said simply.

Divine couldn't speak. It was as if she had been hypnotized. Miriana whistled to the hyenas and they trotted along behind.

Arnold groaned and sat down. 'I mustn't walk any more,' he said. 'I'm having babies and I don't want to tread on them.'

'You're *what*? Arnold, you're a boy. Boy chimps can't have babies.'

'I am,' he insisted. 'Ten babies. Look, they're coming out of my feet. See?'

'Those are your toes, Arnold.'

'They're not babies?'

'No.'

He gave a little sigh and then smiled at me. 'I don't know what I'd do without you, Dinah.'

We walked back to The Dark House. Divine was handed over to the police and the hyenas were taken care of by Animal Rescue. Miriana wanted to know where Mr Peter and the children were. Her face fell when she heard the news. One of the policemen noticed her concern and he opened his car door.

'Hop in,' he said. 'I'll drop you at the hospital. I've got to go past it on my way.' He didn't have to go past the hospital at all, but he was a kind man. He didn't even refuse when Miriana asked if she could take a chimp and a mynah bird with her.

17 Mark: Everyone Should Know This Cure

We were all put into beds at the hospital, three of us in a row. The nurse said it was like looking after the Three Bears. The doctor said it was more like Three Little Pigs. Tammy and I were fine. We were tired and dirty, but the nurses soon sorted us out. It was Dad I worried about.

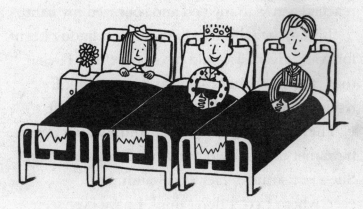

They wouldn't let us see him until they'd cleaned him up. Luckily, he didn't have any broken bones, but he was badly bruised and the cut on his head was pretty impressive. He had nine stitches. He asked the doctor how many buttons they were sewing on!

It all went quiet after that, and I was glad because it gave me time to get something off my mind. 'I'm sorry about all this, Dad.'

'It's not your fault!' Dad seemed surprised.

'It is. If I hadn't put that advert in the Lonely Hearts column, none of this would have happened.'

Dad was silent for a long time. I thought, He's angry. He can't think what to say to me. He's just angry, angry, angry and it's all my fault. Then he reached across to my bed and squeezed my hand.

'Listen,' he whispered at last. 'If it hadn't been for your advert, I would never have met Divine, that's true. I thought she was so beautiful. I really did think she liked me, and I liked her.'

There was another pause. 'And I would never have met the Madwoman from Romania either. She's *very* strange. Her eyes haunt me, everywhere I go. I don't think I have ever seen such dark eyes. But she makes me so cross! I don't suppose I shall see her again.'

It must have been some kind of magic,

because at that moment guess who walked in! The Madwoman from Romania!

'Are you his wife?' asked one of the nurses.

'Not yet,' said Miriana. 'But soon.'

'I'm not marrying you,' cried Dad.

'You be quiet,' Miriana snapped back. 'You sick man. You rest.'

'She's quite right,' agreed the nurse.

'They can go home?' asked Miriana.

'Well, the thing is he should stay in bed for at least three days. Who will look after the children, or indeed Mr Draper himself?'

I started to get out of bed. 'It's all right,' I began. 'I'll keep an eye on Dad. I'm used to organizing everything.'

Dad groaned and began to mutter something under his breath about being saved from a fate worse than death, but I think he was getting feverish. Miriana grabbed my feet and lifted them back on the bed.

'And you, Mr Leopard, you get into bed. Now I in charge.' Dad groaned even louder and began muttering about frying pans and fires. Miriana ignored him and turned to the nurse.

'Is no problem. I look after them.'

'Brilliant!' Tammy whispered to me, and sucked her thumb.

And that is exactly what happened. We were allowed home and Miriana came with us. Dad was put to bed and Miriana made everyone breakfast. Then Tammy and I went to bed and slept and slept and slept.

Over the next few days Dad slowly got better. Miriana wouldn't let him see anyone, not even Miss Pettigrew when she called round. She had a bunch of grapes with her.

'Is he all right? I brought these for him.'

'Is very kind,' nodded Miriana. 'Thank you. Have we met before? At clinic maybe?'

Miss Pettigrew coloured a little. 'No, I don't think so. I thought I might show him my mouse. It's got a bent tail. I found it in my classroom. It's rather sweet. I thought he might like some company. I could sit with him for a bit.'

Miriana smiled. 'Ah, now I understand. You like Vetman!'

'Oh no,' said Miss Pettigrew. 'I prefer Superma– oh! *Vetman!* You mean Mr Draper. Yes, he is very nice, but he's lonely you know and I thought –'

x

Miriana interrupted. 'Listen, I tell you story. Once upon time I meet Vetman and we fall in love and we marry. Then I Mrs Vetman and we have five children and we live happy ever forever. The End.'

'Oh, I see. It's like that,' sighed Miss Pettigrew. 'I'll go home then. Tell me, is that a chimpanzee watching your television?'

'Yes. Is programme about hospitals. He like a lot.'

So life slowly got back to normal, if you can call it normal to live in a house run by a Madwoman from Romania, with a chimpanzee and a much-too-clever mynah bird.

Tamsin made a little gift for Dad to cheer him up. 'It's a crockadipe,' Tammy told him. 'Miriana helped me and the paint doesn't come off and it can't go soggy.'

'I'm very pleased to hear it.'

The police had to come round a couple of times to take statements from Dad and Miriana. That was when we discovered what Miriana had actually done that morning.

'You tamed five wild hyenas?' Dad was astonished.

'So? Is easy.'

'And you hypnotized Divine so that she followed you like a tame lamb? How?'

Miriana shrugged. 'Is old Romanian gift. My grandmother taught me.'

'She's an old Romanian,' I chimed in.

'But hyenas – that's incredible.'

'Listen, Mr Vetman, I was born close to country of Dracula. Is strange place. I can do many things.'

After a couple of days or so, Dad got up and began to wander about, a bit stiffly at first, but he was improving all the time.

'You walk like ostrich,' Miriana told him.

'I do not!'

'Oh yes, is ostrich, like so.' Miriana strutted up and down. Tammy fell about laughing.

'You're an ostrich, Daddy.'

'I am not!' Dad was so cross. He made a real effort *not* to walk like an ostrich. His face suddenly screwed up in pain and he froze on the spot. 'Ow! My back!'

Miriana rushed over and held his arms. 'OK,' she said. 'Now, easy, put your hands on my shoulders like so. Good. Now I put my hands here.' Miriana placed her hands on Dad's waist.

'Are you sure you know what you're doing?' asked Dad, still wincing from the pain. 'I suppose your granny taught you this too?'

'Oh no, even children know this. If you don't, you not so clever. Brain maybe only small space station. This take away all pain. Now, I pull you close like so.' Miriana glanced back over her shoulder. 'You two, close eyes. Go on, close them. That's good, Tammy. And you, Mr Organizer-Leopard-Man, good. Now, I make your father's back better.'

OOH-LALA

There was a long, long silence. I heard Tammy take a sharp little breath and she nudged me, hard. I opened my eyes just as Dinah let out a squawk.

Ooh la la!

18 Mark: The Wedding

The wedding was brilliant. Everyone was dressed up. Dad wore a suit. I had never, ever seen him in a suit before. I was quite proud of him! Miriana looked wonderful. Divine might have been stunningly attractive, but my new mum was beautiful in a very different way. It seemed to come from things that you couldn't actually see, but you knew they were there.

Miriana said she was going to do my hair for the wedding.

'Good,' said Dad. 'Those spots look daft.'

'I like them,' I insisted.

'We change them for wedding,' Miriana said, and Dad grinned at me. I was furious and went stomping out of the room.

Anyhow, a couple of days later Miriana sneaked quietly into my bedroom. 'Now, Mr Leopard. I think is time for change. We do your hairs, eh?'

'I don't want my hair done,' I growled.

Miriana shrugged. 'So, I don't want my hairs done either. You think I like to look like some kind of fashion doll, some Boobie?'

I couldn't help giggling. 'Barbie,' I told her.

'All right, Barbie. But is not me.' She studied me seriously. 'Wedding is important day for all of us. Yes?'

I nodded.

'Everyone go to lot of trouble. We must look good, so we have hairs done.'

I started to say something, but Miriana stopped me. 'I have idea. I think, how we go to wedding? You, me, Tamsin? How we have hairs? Then I have good idea. Wedding is special day, beautiful day, so . . . we go like Birds of Paradise.'

I stared at her. My new mum wanted all three of us to dye our hair so that we looked like Birds of Paradise? Wow!

And that's exactly what we did. Dad almost fainted on the spot! He was so surprised. He really couldn't think of anything to say. He stood there, rocking slightly on his feet, staring at our multicoloured heads with his eyes practically bursting out of their sockets.

Then he smiled, and Tammy laughed and everything was all right. Miriana said that Dinah and Arnold had to come to the wedding too. Dinah sat on Dad's shoulder until she got over-excited and went and sat on his head instead.

As for Arnold, he was the chief bridesmaid! (Julie and Miss Pettigrew were the others, and Miss Pettigrew cried all the way through.) Arnold wore a lovely white dress and a little crown of flowers on his head. He looked quite sweet, except that when the registrar said to

Dad, 'Do you take this woman to be your wife?'
Arnold leaned to one side and parped.

You know how sometimes you want to laugh
and you know you shouldn't because everything
is meant to be serious? It was like that. I was
struggling to stop myself bursting with giggles,
and so were Tammy and Miriana. You'll never
guess who it was that started.

It was Dad! He just couldn't help himself. He
collapsed in a heaving heap of hysterics and of
course that set the rest of us off. Arnold twigged
that he'd done something funny and immediately
stuffed his hand under his armpit and began
pumping. *Splurrrgh! Splurrrgh!* Even the registrar
was rolling about. It was a fabulous day!

We had a party back at our house and
Sanjeev and his family came and friends of Dad
and Miriana. As soon as Sanjeev saw me he
fished about in his pockets and eventually pulled
out a matchbox.

'I got you a wedding present,' he said.

'But it's not my wedding!'

'I know, but I thought why should the bride
and groom get everything? So I got something
especially for you.'

161

'That's really kind, Sanjeev. Thanks.'

I pushed open the little box. Inside was a small bit of twig. 'What is it?'

'A stick insect.'

'It's a twig.'

'No, it's a stick insect, but its legs have fallen off.'

'Sanjeev!'

He shrugged happily. 'Well, I don't suppose anyone else has ever given you a present like that, so it's very special, and it's from me.'

'You're an idiot.'

'Takes one to know one,' he said with a grin.

Miriana had done nearly all the cooking (with some help from Tammy) and the food was fabulous. I'd asked her to make some custard as a special treat.

IT HAD LUMPS IN IT! Even Dinah made a song and dance about it. She flew round and round the room squawking, 'Custard! Make custard!'

So not everything is quite perfect yet. But we're all back home and settling down and getting used to each other. It feels strange now, but probably in a year or two it won't seem odd at all. It will be like this has always been our family, all six of us – Dad, Miriana-Mum, Tammy, Dinah, Arnold and me.

Happy ever forever? Wait and see.

Dinah's Epilogue

The clinic door banged open and in came a
spotty girl and a man, with a stretcher between
them. Another man was lying face down on the
stretcher with what looked like a large brown
accident stuck on his back. Mr Peter was speechless.

'It's me dachshund, Chantelle,' said the girl
with a sniff. 'She's stuck again.'

I was rammed against the bars of my cage,
trying to work out what had been going on. It
was quite a puzzle. I could just about see a
splattered sausage shape spread across the man's
back, but that was all.

'Wuff,' said the splatter shape.

'She went for me,' complained the man on
the stretcher. 'Wasn't my fault. She leaped on my
back and now she's stuck there.'

Mr Peter ran his fingers over the back of the
man's coat. 'Good heavens! Your coat's made of
Velcro!'

'That's right. I'm known as Mr Gecko. I run a fairground attraction. You wear Velcro pads and hurl yourself at the wall and stick there, like a fly. I was getting ready for a demonstration event when this hairy sausage comes hurtling across the field and leaps up at me. I turned my back on her and now she's stuck there. Stupid animal!'

'She thought you were a rabbit,' sniffed the girl.

A rabbit? I fell off my perch, laughing. I couldn't help it. I just lay on my back on the floor of my cage, plucking the air helplessly with my claws and gasping for breath.

HA HA HA

'Do I look like a rabbit?' demanded the man on the stretcher.

'I meant a squirrel.'

A squirrel? Oh, please! Someone help me! I was dying of laughter. I thought I'd shake every feather from my body. Even Mr Peter was desperately trying to keep a straight face.

'Well, you're definitely like a hedgehog,' the girl went on defiantly.

'Wuff,' went the claggy brown mess.

Mr Peter fetched a pair of scissors. He helped the man to sit up and began to cut the dog free. 'I'm afraid her coat will look a bit of a mess for a while, but in time it will grow back.' At last he lifted the dog clear. What a sight! She had semi-bald patches all over her. The girl gave Mr Gecko a haughty glare, sniffed loudly and swept from the room.

'They're a right pair, they are,' muttered Mr Gecko. He scowled across at me. 'What's that bird doing? Is she laughing?'

Laughing? Oh yes! I laughed so much I wet myself. *Excusez-moi!*

Tail-piece:
No animals (or humans) were hurt during the
writing of this story.

LAUGH YOUR SOCKS OFF WITH Jeremy STRONG

Jeremy Strong has written SO many books to make you laugh your socks right off. There are the Streaker books and the Famous Bottom books and the Pyjamas books and ... PHEW!

Welcome to the JEREMY STRONG FAMILY TREE, which shows you all of Jeremy's brilliant books in one easy-to-follow-while-laughing-your-socks-off way!

MY BROTHER'S FAMOUS BOTTOM
Nicholas's baby brother, Cheese, is famous. Well, his bottom is, because he advertises Dumper disposable nappies ...

Woofy hi! I'm Streaker, the fastest dog in the world. My owner, Trevor, thinks he can train me to obey him. The trouble is even I don't know what I'm going to do next! I don't know what **SIT** or **STOP** mean, and I do get into some big scrapes. We almost got arrested once! This is the first book about me and it's almost as funny and fast as I am!

LAUGH YOUR SOCKS OFF WITH

THE HUNDRED-MILE-AN-HOUR DOG

Available Now!

* * * * * * * * * * * * * * * * * * *

I'm Jamie. I am going to be the world's greatest film director when I grow up. I'm trying to make a film about a cartoon cow I've invented called **KRAZY KOW**. However, making a film isn't as easy as you might think. How was I to know everyone would see the bit where I caught my big sister snogging Justin? How was I to know the exploding strawberries would make quite so much mess? How was I to know my big bro's football kit would turn pink? And why did everyone have to blame ME?

LAUGH YOUR SOCKS OFF WITH

KRAZY KOW SAVES THE WORLD – WELL, ALMOST

Available Now!

14½ Things You Didn't Know About

Jeremy Strong

★ ★ ★ ★ ★ ★ ★ ★ ★ ★ ★ ★ ★ ★ ★ ★ ★

1. He loves eating liquorice.

2. He used to like diving. He once dived from the high board and his trunks came off!

3. He used to play electric violin in a rock band called **THE INEDIBLE CHEESE SANDWICH**.

4. He got a 100-metre swimming certificate when he couldn't even swim.

5. When he was five, he sat on a heater and burnt his bottom.

6. Jeremy used to look after a dog that kept eating his underpants. (No – **NOT** while he was wearing them!)

7. When he was five, he left a basin tap running with the plug in and flooded the bathroom.

8. He can make his ears waggle.

9. He has visited over a thousand schools.

10. He once scored minus ten in an exam! That's ten less than nothing!

11. His hair has gone grey, but his mind hasn't.

12. He'd like to have a pet tiger.

13. He'd like to learn the piano.

14. He has dreadful handwriting.

And a half . . . His favourite hobby is sleeping. He's very good at it.

There's no point in writing twenty pages of boring rubbish if you can produce two pages of finely tooled, engaging story.

Of all the books you have written, which is your favourite?

I loved writing both **KRAZY KOW SAVES THE WORLD – WELL, ALMOST** and **STUFF**, my first book for teenagers. Both these made me laugh out loud while I was writing and I was pleased with the overall result in each case. I also love writing the stories about Nicholas and his daft family – **MY DAD**, **MY MUM**, **MY BROTHER** and so on.

If you couldn't be a writer what would you be?

Well, I'd be pretty fed up for a start, because writing was the one thing I knew I wanted to do from the age of nine onward. But if I DID have to do something else, I would love to be either an accomplished pianist or an artist of some sort. Music and art have played a big part in my whole life and I would love to be involved in them in some way.

What's the best thing about writing stories?

Oh dear – so many things to say here! Getting paid for making things up is pretty high on the list! It's also something you do on your own, inside your own head – nobody can interfere with that. The only boss you have is yourself. And you are creating something that nobody else has made before you. I also love making my readers laugh and want to read more and more.

Did you ever have nightmare teacher? (And who was your best ever?)

My nightmare at primary school was Mrs Chappell, long since dead. I knew her secret – she was not actually human. She was a Tyrannosaurus rex in disguise. She taught me for two years when I was in Y5 and Y6, and we didn't like each other at all. My best ever was when I was in Y3 and Y4. Her name was Miss Cox, and she was the one who first encouraged me to write stories. She was brilliant. Sadly, she is long since dead too.

When you were a kid you used to play kiss-chase. Did you always do the chasing or did anyone ever chase you?!

I usually did the chasing, but when I got chased, I didn't bother to run very fast! Maybe I shouldn't admit to that! We didn't play kiss-chase at school – it was usually played during the holidays. If we had tried playing it at school we would have been in serious trouble. Mind you, I seemed to spend most of my time in trouble of one sort or another, so maybe it wouldn't have mattered that much.

Ask Jeremy

What's your favourite book/film/song?

I have many favourite books but one of my best when I was a teenager was **MY FAMILY AND OTHER ANIMALS**, by Gerald Durrell. I always liked animal stories as a child and the combination of animal observation and him gazing at his strange family as they while away their time on a fabulous Mediterranean island was hugely engaging and funny.

When did you start writing?

I have long stories I wrote when I was six, but I didn't really get under way until my middle teens, when I started writing poetry. I'd come across the poems of Dylan Thomas and fell in love with his wordplay and the sheer music of his poems. I decided I would be the next Dylan Thomas. Obviously things didn't quite work out like that in the end, but it was the beginning!

Where do your ideas and inspirations come from?

If only I knew! It's a case of trying to be open and alive to experiences, events, sights, sounds, feelings and so on. I keep notebooks, of course, and write things down, but very few of my notes end up being turned into stories. I can't force ideas to pop into my head.

My three tips for becoming a successful author

1. Make sure your main characters are strongly portrayed and interesting. They will help you write the story. Don't have too many important characters because you will find it difficult to keep track of them throughout the story.

2. Always try to put in the unexpected. It could be a character detail, e.g. one of them has a glass eye, or is an expert at rabbit-skinning. It could be something that happens or a bit of great description. Such 'events' keep the reader hooked and wanting to read on.

3. Always read your work out loud to yourself. It's a really good way to get a feel for your work. You also notice where you've made mistakes, repeated yourself and where what you've written sounds boring. You can then rewrite so the story gets better. And remember that 'longer' usually means 'not so good'!

JOKE BOOKS
You'll never be stuck for a joke to share again.

THE HUNDRED-MILE-AN-HOUR DOG
Streaker is no ordinary dog; she's a rocket on four legs with a woof attached . . .

COSMIC PYJAMAS
Pyjamas are just pyjamas, right? Not when they're COSMIC PYJAMAS, swooooosh! . . .

COWS, CARTOONS, ELEPHANTS AND . . . ORANG-UTANS?!
Warning – may induce red cheeks and tears of laughter!